HALLOWS END

A CURSE OF THE BLOOD MOON NOVEL

KRISTEN PROBY

&
AMPERSAND
PUBLISHING, INC.

Hallows End
A Curse of the Blood Moon Novel
by
Kristen Proby

HALLOWS END

A Curse of the Blood Moon Novel

Kristen Proby

Cover Design: By Hang Le

This series is dedicated to my great-aunt,
Kathy E. Paul.
She loved my paranormal stories the most, and was so
incredibly proud of me that she beamed with it.
I miss you, Kath. We didn't have enough time.
And I love you more.

PROLOGUE
JONAS

September 1692

"They took Margaret Scott."

I look up into the sad eyes of my long-time friend, my coven sister, Louisa, and feel my heart sink with sadness.

"They will execute them," she continues, her voice full of frustration and urgency. "Jonas, we must do something."

"If we speak up, we expose the entire coven, and they will murder us all," I reply and feel the candles around us flaming higher, fueled by my anger. "We cannot risk hundreds of lives, Louisa."

"So the few shall die instead?" she insists. "Those women have been good to us, Jonas. They have not done anything wrong, and they are certainly *not* witches. Margaret has worked tirelessly to protect us, to *conceal* us from their unjust government."

"I know." I stand and cross to Louisa, laying my hand on her shoulder. Her aura swirls in outrage. "And I am eternally grateful to her. To all of them. Would you have me send our entire family to slaughter now? Because if I go forward and defend Margaret, that is what will transpire."

She shakes her head, tightening her lips in despair. "It is not right."

"No. It is not. Staying silent as they punish our allies is wrong. But I do not know what else to do."

She turns away and then looks back at me. "I have been dreaming again. I suspect that it will not matter in the end, regardless of whether we speak up now or not. I see fire. I hear screams. They will come for Hallows End, Jonas. It is only a matter of time. Did you see the blood on the moon this night?"

The thought sends terror through me, and I know she's right.

I've had the same dreams.

And I saw the blood on the moon.

"Jonas, you know that what I say is true!"

"I know." My voice is rough with grief—with resignation. "You are right. It is time. Summon the others."

"We cannot undo it once the spell is cast," she warns me.

"The alternative is death," I remind her. "Assemble in

the town square in one hour. We will end this bloodshed and protect our own."

"Will I remember?" she asks. "When it is finished, and we are safe, will we know what we did?"

"No. Only I will remember. It is as it should be."

"The burden is too great—"

"Go," I interrupt. "Make haste. Time runs out."

She pauses and hurries over to hug me close. "I'm sorry, brother."

"It is what is meant," I say and pat her back. "Now, do as I ask, won't you?"

"Yes." She wipes at a tear on her cheek. "Yes, I will make the preparations."

She hurries out of my small, modest house, and I return to my desk, opening the bottom drawer to retrieve my Book of Shadows.

It's time to cast the curse of the blood moon.

CHAPTER ONE
LUCY

I don't like the dreams. I've never been a fan of them, even as a child when I knew what my birthday presents would be or where we'd spend our spring vacations. But the dreams—visions, really—have never been frightening. Just informative.

Still, let me tell you, when a woman is blessed with the gift of precognition, it's hard to surprise her with much of anything.

Lately, however, the dreams have turned darker. Are they indicative of what *will* be or what *may* be? That's the question I've never been able to answer—and the one I fear the most.

After another night of fitful sleep and disturbing dreams, I rolled out of bed early to go outside where I feel most at peace.

"Come on, Nera, let's go tend the garden."

My Irish wolfhound, with his shaggy, dark gray coat

and happy disposition, follows me through the kitchen and out the back door to our garden. Most of what I sell in my apothecary comes from this plot. There are some things I can't grow, very few things I have to send away for, but for the most part, I lovingly and carefully tend to it all right here.

As I walk down the steps, the flowers open to greet me.

"Good morning," I murmur with a soft smile, a mug of coffee clutched in one hand and a basket for gathering in the other. "You got some rain last night, I see. It's good for you."

I walk farther down the path, and more flowers open as if waking from a long nap. I can almost hear them yawn, and it makes me smile softly.

Nera jogs over to the far corner of the grassy yard to do his business, knowing better than to relieve himself on any of the flowers.

Good boy, I say to him with my mind.

His head comes up, and he offers me a wide doggie grin, his tongue hanging out of his mouth. Nera's been with me for just over five years. He was a stray and hadn't known a gentle touch before mine. But he found me, and I knew as soon as I locked eyes with him that he was mine.

The shop is running low on lavender and rosemary, which isn't surprising. Those sell the quickest because whether a person is a newbie witch just feeling out their power or rooted in the Craft for their entire lives, those two herbs are essential to any witch's cabinet. So, I kneel in the dirt and get to work on the lavender. Thanks to the greenhouse I built two years ago, I can keep the herbs growing at different stages and never run out.

The air this morning has a chill indicative of October, and I know that it won't be too long before I'm working exclusively in the greenhouse.

I glance at the smaller plants that I put in the ground just last week and eye them speculatively.

They could use an extra inch or two. At this rate, I'll be harvesting them next week, and the frost could come at any time.

So, with a wave of my fingers, the plants lighten in color and grow to a height that pleases me.

"That'll work," I murmur in satisfaction.

The sound of Nera growling has me frowning and looking over my shoulder. He's standing at full attention near the picket fence in need of new white paint, the hair on his back standing up.

What is it, boy?

He looks at me and then back out into the woods once more.

The wind moves as I stand and reach out with my mind, searching for what Nera senses, but all I see is a small family of deer.

Just some deer.

He looks at me once more and whimpers, so I set my basket down and walk his way. When my hand settles on his back, I can feel the hum of energy vibrating through him.

Something spooked him.

I search with my mind once more. It's only just daylight, the sun still waking up over the ocean and casting everything in golden light. The trees sway in the breeze, their leaves just beginning to turn yellow. I take a deep breath and send my mind's eye high above those trees to peer down below.

"Nothing," I murmur aloud. "I only see the deer, Nera."

But I pick some dill, oregano, and parsley to add to the rosemary and sprinkle it along the fence line to reinforce the protection spell I work each Saturday to keep my property safe from anything negative.

"We have to pick some chamomile for Breena."

Nera's head whirls around at the mention of my cousin's name, whatever he thought he heard or saw before forgotten. I'm convinced my familiar has a bit of a crush on Breena.

"She'll be here in a little while," I continue as I add the yellow flowers to my basket. "We'll have a nice visit with her before we open the shop for the day."

Nera shuffles his big feet in excitement, and I lean over to plant a kiss on his cheek.

"I know, Breena's your favorite—besides me, of course." I kiss him again. "Right?"

Nera nuzzles my shoulder.

"I thought so. Come on. We have to get these into the oven to dry."

I already preheated the oven, so I gently lay the blooms on their trays and slide them onto the racks, then pour myself another mug of coffee, stir in the creamer, and head for the bedroom to dress for the day.

I'm partial to greens and orange and pull a flowy orange dress from the closet. Customers expect to see the witch of the house dressing the part, and it's lucky for them that I enjoy feminine clothes with an edgy, mystical look to them.

I tease my long, red hair into a braid, weave twine with bells into it for fun and cleansing, and then slide my feet into my shoes, just as I hear Breena's voice call out for me.

Nera immediately abandons me for her, and I smile as I follow him out to the kitchen.

"Good morning," I say with a laugh as Nera rubs himself against Breena, almost knocking her over.

"Hi," she says and scratches Nera's side until I think he might lie down in sheer happiness. "And good morning to you, sweet boy. I brought you a goody. Yes, I did."

Breena comes over at least twice a week to stock up on things for her practice and leaves behind gifts in exchange. We worked out this barter system years ago.

There are three of us first cousins, all girls, and of the three of us, Breena is the brightest. The innocent one. She is the epitome of a hearth witch, always at the ready to take care of us all. She makes her wares out of love as well as plants, fibers, and elbow grease.

"I'm trying out a new syrup," Breena informs me and pulls a tall bottle from her bag, setting it on the counter. "It has honeysuckle. I think you'll like it. And for my favorite boy, I made peanut butter treats."

Nera whimpers in excitement and sits with the manners of a gentleman as he waits for his biscuit.

"He has you wrapped around his huge paw," I inform her dryly and take a sip of my coffee. "Need some caffeine?"

"Yes, please," she says happily and boosts herself onto the stool by the kitchen island. She gazes around the room and then smiles at me.

"What?"

"I never know what to expect when I come in here," she says with a shrug. "Some days, you have roses or sunflowers hanging upside down to dry. Other times, you have herbs in the oven."

"Like today."

Breena nods, sips her coffee, and then wrinkles her nose and reaches for my sugar bowl. She ladles in two teaspoons and then sets the spoon to stirring clockwise—without using her hands.

I smile and wonder what her stirring deasil is meant to bring to her.

"I've always loved your kitchen," she continues with a sigh and rests her chin on her hand. "It's warm, and it smells good."

"How's the ivy seedling I sent home with you last week?"

Her smile falls, and she looks down into her coffee.

"*Breena.*"

"You're the green witch," she reminds me. "And you *know* that I'm hopeless when it comes to plants. I can knit you a sweater or bake you a pie, but I can't keep green things alive."

"Bring it over. I'll save it," I reply and lean against the counter. "You're the one who said you'd like a plant for your mantel. Ivy is practically impossible to kill."

"Well, if you ever need to have some offed, I'm your girl," she says. "I have a question."

"Shoot."

"Have you been dreaming?"

I meet her eyes and sigh. "You know that I always dream."

"I know, but I don't. Not that I can ever remember," Breena replies with an answering sigh. "But I have been. I don't remember everything, only bits and pieces, but they terrify me, Lucy. I don't know *what* is scaring me, exactly, but I wake up shaking, frightened, and so cold that it takes thirty minutes in a hot shower to warm up."

"You don't remember anything specific about the dreams?" I ask as I hurry around the island to wrap my arms around my cousin and hold her close.

"I hear laughter," she whispers against my shoulder. "But the kind that turns your bones to ice."

"Yeah." I sigh and brush my fingers through her faerie-blond hair. "I hear it, too."

Nera's head comes up off the bed he's been curled up on. He tilts it to the side and whines, his eyes pinned to the door.

"Is someone here?" Breena asks. I hate that I can hear fear in her voice.

"I wasn't expecting her so soon." I rub circles on Breena's back and watch the entryway, knowing exactly who's arrived.

I knew she would come, eventually.

"Who?"

But before I can answer, a quick knock sounds on the door, and Lorelei comes through it with a bright smile on her gorgeous face.

"Surprise."

"Oh, my goddess!" Breena jumps up and rushes to tackle-hug our cousin. "You're here! You haven't come home in...I don't even know how long."

"Three years," I finish for her and smile at Lorelei over Breena's shoulder. The air pulses around us the way it always does when the three of us are together.

We are the daughters of daughters, witches who can trace our lineage back to the beginning of recorded history here in our little part of Massachusetts. Long before the witch trials that killed people who weren't witches at all.

"Hi," Lorelei says, uncertainty weighing in those gorgeous green eyes.

"Welcome," I reply and wrap my arms around them both, holding on tightly. I had no idea until this moment how badly I needed this, the power of the three of us together.

"How long are you here?" Breena asks. "A week? Two?"

"Maybe forever," Lorelei replies, surprising us both.

"What happened to teaching folklore at that fancy university in California?" I ask, taking in Lorelei's jeans and simple white T-shirt. "Are you wearing *Nikes*?"

"They're comfortable," she says with a shrug. "If I wear my dresses and cloaks in LA, I get funny looks."

"You're a folklore professor from Salem," Breena points out. "I don't think it would be weird at all. But you always had an ass for denim."

"Thanks." Lorelei grins and turns to show off said ass. "I've been doing a lot of lunges."

"Nice," Breena says with a nod. "They're working. I've been trying to build my arm muscles for kneading bread and all the cast iron lifting I do."

"Good idea," Lorelei says. "I've missed your bread *so* much."

"As much as I love this conversation about fitness, perhaps we could discuss what brings Lorelei home after she said, repeatedly, that she'd pretty much *never* come home to stay."

"Did I say *never*?"

"'*I'm never living in Salem again*' is pretty much word for word what you said," Breena agrees.

"Well, you know, plans change." Lorelei shrugs and runs her hand over Nera's head, not looking either of us in the eyes.

Breena and I share a look.

"Xander still lives here," Breena says gently.

"I'm *not* here for him," Lorelei snaps in defense with immediate heat. "This has nothing to do with him. I'm a grown adult, capable of living in the same town as *him*."

"Of course, you are," I agree with a nod, and Breena and I share another look.

"I've been dreaming," Lorelei finally admits with a long sigh and pours herself a cup of coffee, adding both cream and sugar and stirring clockwise. "At first, I thought they were just simple dreams, that they meant nothing except that I shouldn't eat lavender ice cream before bed."

"The dairy will kill you," Breena advises.

"But it's not the ice cream," I add, already knowing what she's been dreaming.

"No." Lorelei meets my gaze. "It's not. Something's happening, and while I don't know *what* it is, I do know that I'm needed here. So, here I am. I'll be living in Mom's cottage by the shore."

"Good. She has wanted you to live there for years. You're a sea witch, Lorelei. You belong in that house."

"I admit, I'm excited to be there." Her voice is soft, but she glances at us with an excited grin and a twinkle in her beautiful green eyes. "I haven't been honing my skills.

I've been doing the bare minimum since I left, and that was on purpose."

"I know," Breena and I say at the same time.

What Lorelei went through was...intense.

"I can't walk away from my Craft," she admits. "I know that now, and I feel like I'm bursting at the seams to start practicing again."

"I'm so damn happy for you," I reply and hug her close once more. "You're too powerful to suppress who you are, cousin."

"She had to learn that for herself," Breena adds. "I'm so happy you're home. We've missed you terribly."

"Thank you. I need some supplies. Herbs, oils, candles. Crystals."

Breena giggles, and I smile widely.

"Lucky for you, we know where you can get all those things and more."

"And you're just in time for Samhain," Breena says, jumping in excitement. "And the Harvest Moon. They're on the same day this year, so we're celebrating all week. The moms have been having a field day with all the plans for the coven."

Several emotions play over Lorelei's face. Excitement, caution, concern, and then happiness again.

"Don't worry," I say. "It'll be fun. And good for you spiritually. It'll give you the boost you need."

"*He'll* be there, though," she whispers.

"That'll be good for you, too," Breena says. "Don't

worry. We'll work some protection spells before you have to see him to keep your heart safe."

"I don't know if any spell can keep me safe from him." Lorelei shrugs. "I've tried that. But I'll be okay. It's time I'm with my family again."

———

I wake with a start and look at the time.

Three in the morning.

Of course.

My lips twist at the irony of another horrible dream tearing me out of sleep at the witching hour, and I sit up to wipe the tears from my cheeks. Why am I so unbearably sad? I heard the sinister laughter, the cries of help, and saw the horrendous darkness.

I don't know what to do to stop any of it.

Nera sleeps on his bed next to mine, and when I reach out, I see that it's a peaceful sleep, so I decide to leave him in bed and go outside to let the fresh air clear the darkness from my mind.

The garden soothes me. It always has. My mother would find me curled up in a bed of forget-me-nots or under the massive willow tree in the backyard many mornings. I didn't run to her bed when I was troubled; I ran outside. At first, that terrified her, but then she learned it was my path. This is my safety.

And she cultivated it within me, taught me how to harness the power, how to show my gratitude to the deities and acknowledge the responsibilities that come with my gifts.

Goddess, how I miss her.

Barefoot and dressed only in a flowing green robe, I walk out into the night. My moonflowers are open and reaching for the moon. The sky is clear, and I search for the Sagittarius constellation.

The air is still tonight. I hear a dog barking across town and the water lapping at the shoreline less than a mile from where I'm standing.

Spirits walk through Salem at night, the way the living do during the day. I can sense them, especially as we near Samhain when the veil between the worlds of the living and the dead is the thinnest. But they don't frighten me. I'm well protected, and they mean me no harm in any case.

I take a long, deep, cleansing breath and let it out slowly, already feeling much better. Suddenly, I see the glimmer of soft, yellow light in the trees.

Fireflies?

"Awfully bright for lightning bugs," I murmur softly and step forward to get a better look. The light is building, growing as it moves steadily through the trees, and then I see that it's a *man*.

Without thinking, I step through the garden gate and follow him through the woods. He's walking quickly, but not as though he's running to or from anything. I want to catch him and ask who he is and what he's doing. The air is cool on my skin as I hurry after him, and I barely notice the scrapes and pokes in the soles of my feet from the underbrush.

He stops at the small wooden walking bridge that stretches over the creek at the edge of my property and looks back at me. He seems surprised to see me, and I call out to him.

"Wait. Can I help you?"

I don't know why I think that he *needs* my aid, but it's the first thing that comes out of my mouth. My energy is so focused on him, so weirdly hell-bent on contacting him, that even the branches of the trees around me reach for him.

Without answering, he turns and crosses the bridge. Once on the other side, he's simply...*gone.*

The light blinks out as if flicked off by a switch, and I'm standing by the bridge in the dark.

"What in the world?" I ask softly as I turn back toward home. "Am I losing my mind?"

When I get back to the garden gate, I can hear Nera barking inside the house, and I immediately reach out to him.

I'm okay! I hurry inside and fall to my knees to hug him close. "I'm okay, baby."

He's whimpering and sniffing me as if he has to make sure for himself that I'm safe.

"I know I shouldn't have gone without you. It was the...oddest experience, and we both know that I've seen some wild shit."

He whimpers once more and sits in front of me, holding my gaze with his.

"I'm safe, Nera."

He presses his face to mine.

"I'm sorry that I worried you. Come on, let's go back to bed."

But neither of us goes back to sleep. We lie in bed, Nera with me now rather than on his bed, and we listen to the night around us filtering in through the open windows. Night birds call, and I hear the ships in the harbor.

But I can't get the man's glowing light and blue eyes out of my head. It's as though I'm *supposed* to know him, but I've never seen him before.

Not even in my dreams.

I'm not easy to surprise. I see too much.

But this has me shocked to my core, and I have a million questions.

___

My mother may be dead, but that doesn't mean I can't talk to her. I'm just not a medium, so I can't *hear* her.

I need the aunts for that.

Lorelei's and Breena's moms, Astrid and Hilda, live in a cottage outside of town near the sea. They moved in together several years ago with my mother when they all decided it was high time they were old witches together for the rest of their days.

If you look up *eccentric witch* in the dictionary, a photo of the three of them would likely be there.

It's early, just past dawn, when Nera and I walk through their gate and up the steps to the old house. Roses and ivy climb the outside of the building, and it just *looks* like something old witches would live in.

It's absolutely divine and totally life goals for when Breena, Lorelei, and I are old ladies.

"Good morning, darling girl," Astrid says with a smile as she opens the door. "We're having strawberry rhubarb pie for breakfast."

I raise an eyebrow and immediately feel calmer and safe. "Count me in."

Hilda's in the kitchen, cutting three slices of the pie and setting them on plates.

"The coffee's hot," Hilda says and gestures to a mug on the counter. "Help yourself. What a lovely thing to have one of our girls visit so early."

"I had an odd experience," I say as I pour the coffee, set the spoon to stirring, and accept a plate from Hilda. "And I need to tell you about it."

Nera has already curled up under the table, hoping for one of us to drop some crumbs.

"We love odd experiences," Astrid says with excitement and claps her hands with glee. She has her long, gray hair pulled up into a messy bun on the top of her head this morning. "Tell us everything."

And so, I do. I tell them all about the dreams and walking out to the garden to find the man in the woods. By the time I finish, I realize that none of us has eaten any pie, and the aunts are watching me very closely.

A door closes in the other room.

"Yes, it's beginning," Astrid whispers.

"Is that Mom?" I ask and immediately try to open my mind, to *will* myself to hear her.

"Of course, it is," Hilda says and holds my hand in understanding. "She may not be here physically anymore, but she still lives here all the same. Still as bossy as ever, too."

"Is the man I saw last night in the woods the same one who killed her?" The words come out in a rush.

"No," Astrid replies immediately, then seems to listen to someone speaking in her ear. "Darling, you know that a witch is killed in Salem every year. It's been that way for *hundreds* of years."

"I know," I whisper. "We all live in constant fear of it. Last year, it was *my* mother who paid that horrible price."

"But it wasn't the man you saw," Hilda says. "We can't tell you much more. Honestly, I thought all of this was nothing more than legend."

"It's true," Astrid disagrees. "And it's begun. You're about to take the journey you've been training for all your life. To be successful, it will take all three of you, plus the others you bring along the way. Trust yourselves.

Listen to your guides and your ancestors. They won't lead you astray."

"This sounds *so* ominous. Or like a Marvel movie."

They both smile.

"It's much, much better, darling one," Hilda says. "Or, it could be the ruin of us all."

Nera whimpers under the table.

"No pressure or anything," I mutter.

CHAPTER TWO
JONAS

She saw me.

It's actually not unusual for the townspeople of Salem to see and interact with me, as I've gone into town often over the past three hundred and thirty years, but I went under the cloak of darkness last night. I needed a walk to gather my thoughts and try to set my mind at ease.

But my mind is never at *ease.*

It hasn't been for the entirety of those three-hundred-plus years.

With that said, I don't know why I think that taking a simple walk at night will work to soothe my soul, but I try all the same—and often.

I've never been spotted as I move between worlds before.

Until her.

With flaming red hair, porcelain skin lit up in the

moonlight, and a green robe that billowed around her, she looked like something I might have conjured in my mind.

Something I would have wished for a hundred times over.

A wish that I knew could never come to be.

And yet, there she was, and I was pulled to her as though I knew her. As though my *soul* knew hers. It was a visceral reaction that left me shaken all night and well into the morning.

Is it possible that a change is coming?

I'm hesitant to let myself hope. I'd had no idea all those years ago when I assured Louisa that everything would be okay, that we'd still be caught up in the curse centuries later.

If I had known, would I have taken the same path?

It's a question I've asked myself many times, and I never have a definitive answer.

Because I just don't know how all of this will end.

It's early in the day as I walk through Hallows End. We live under constant cloud cover, casting the village in a dreary, gray pall. I'm the only one from Hallows End to have seen the sun since 1692. The clouds occasionally part some nights so we can see the moon and stars, but even those moments are fleeting.

It frustrates me to no end that I've seen the changes in technology and know the people I care about work harder than they need to. We have no running water, no electricity, and no refrigeration. Those things alone would ease the burdens of this village tremendously.

But I can't tell them about any of it.

And even if I did, it wouldn't matter. They would forget everything by the next new moon anyway.

"Brother Jonas," Louisa says with a happy smile and a wave. She's holding a bushel of lavender, freshly picked from her garden. "The herbs and flowers are still growing so well this autumn. I know that we all grow weary of the gloomy sky and rain, but the crops are happy."

"'Tis been a rainy autumn to be sure," I agree, as I always do. Goddess, how I miss her. How I wish I was able to confide in her the way I once could. "You are right. The crops will thrive with the added moisture. Your lavender is beautiful."

"Chamomile and parsley are coming along, as well," she says with a nod. "I'll make some more parsley oil for you and the apothecary. The Stebbins boy had an earache two weeks past, and I would not want any infection to return."

"I know Mrs. Stebbins will be grateful," I reply. "Thank you, Louisa."

I wave and smile as I pass through the village. I walk this same path every morning, making sure that nothing has changed. That everything is as it should be.

"Good morning, Jonas," Alistair Goode says with a warm smile. Alistair is the town mayor *and* the Christian minister. As such, I stay on his good side, but I do not trust him. There was a time that he would have led a mob to hang me—and others like me.

"Alistair," I say with a nod. "Good day."

I continue through town, and when I'm sure that nothing is amiss, I let my shoulders relax.

"Are you looking for something in particular today, Jonas?"

My heart stutters at the sound of Alistair's voice behind me, but I school my features and turn to the other man with a congenial smile.

"Not at all. I am just out for a walk to take in the fresh air before we get more rain."

He nods and then stares up into the sky. "I pray the clouds part soon and that God will favor us with the sun."

"As do I," I reply before tipping my hat to him and continuing on my way toward my cabin.

But once inside, I'm even more restless. I don't want to be in my home, reading and researching to no avail.

"You want to see *her*," I mutter in frustration. "And that is fruitless."

But unwilling to fight the impulse, I leave once more and walk to the edge of town—to the bridge that takes me between times.

I leave Hallows End, and by the time I'm on the other side of the small bridge, I'm in Salem.

Or, on the edge of it at least, in a little patch of woods near the neighborhood that leads to downtown.

Each time I pass through, I'm somehow magically

dressed to fit the times. I don't keep a home here with a wardrobe.

The clothes just...*change.*

I look to my left. I've always been drawn to the house at the edge of the woods with its picket fence and lovely gardens. Even long ago, when the curse was first cast, and I learned that I could travel between the two worlds, the house called to me. It looked different then, and has been changed and modernized many times over the years, but the footprint is the same.

The garden is the same.

Now, an apothecary is attached to the house, but I haven't taken the time to go inside.

I walk up the steps, and my skin begins to hum.

I open the door, and it's like stepping through an energy field. Every fiber of my being is on high alert, and I smile when a large hound ambles over to give me a sniff.

"Hello there," I murmur and squat to his level. His eyes meet mine, and I know immediately that he's linked to the shop owner.

I wonder if they know that this is their familiar.

"That's Nera. He's friendly," a voice calls from another room. "I'll be right out. Feel free to look around."

"Thank you," I reply and scratch the dog behind his ears.

It smells lovely in here, of rose and mint and lavender. The selection of herbs is impressive, and I must admit, I haven't seen this kind of collection of salves and tinctures in Salem in over a hundred years.

The proprietor knows her business.

Louisa would love it.

"Sorry about that."

The woman from last night hurries out, carrying a large tray of dried flowers and blowing a strand of red hair out of her eyes.

"Please, let me help."

I rush over and take the tray, setting it on the table she gestures to before turning to gaze at her.

I'm immediately pulled to her. It's all I can do to keep six feet of distance between us. I want to reach for her and pull her against me.

I can honestly say this is something entirely new for me.

"I'm Lucy," she says with a forced smile before clearing her throat and jerking away as if she, too, feels the pull. "I'm the owner here. I'd be happy to help with anything you may need. Is there something specific you're looking for?"

I believe I just found it. Despite not looking for it at all.

"Do you carry parsley oil?"

Her smile is wide and immediate. "Oh, yes. It's a great antibiotic, but you must already know that. If you're feeling unwell, you can put a few drops in your mouth. Sore ear? A few drops in the canal will do the trick. It's a lifesaver."

I wander around the shop, taking it all in and trying

to tame the unexplained pull. I can feel the magic in here, and it's like coming home.

"Do I know you?" Lucy asks and walks around a shelf to better see me.

"I don't think so. I'm not from Salem."

She starts to reach for me but pulls her hand back at the last second, cradling it against her chest as her eyes widen. "Oh, my goddess. You're *him.*"

"I'm not sure I know what you're talking about."

"Yes, you do. You're the man I saw walking through the forest last night," she says impatiently as she narrows her spectacular green eyes at me. "It was you."

I take a deep breath and let it out slowly, trying to keep myself under control. I've never felt the kind of pull, the kind of connection, that I feel to this woman in all my life.

For the first time in centuries, I'm out of my element.

"What's your name?" she asks.

"Jonas," I reply.

"What were you doing in the woods last night?" The question is soft, not accusatory, but most definitely curious. "And where did you go when you disappeared?"

"Are you certain you weren't dreaming?"

Her lips firm in frustration. "Trust me, that wasn't a dream. I'm well aware of the difference."

But rather than push and question me further, she turns her attention to the tray of herbs on the nearby table. She talks as she begins sorting the dried blossoms, putting some in glass jars and others in a bucket.

"I'm not used to finding strange men in my woods," she says and lifts a blossom to her nose to sniff. "Strangers, on the other hand, *that* I'm used to. I've lived and worked in Salem all my life, and we get more than our share of tourists wanting to have a paranormal experience; to meet a real witch and maybe get spooked just a little."

"And have I?" I ask as I continue watching her beautiful hands.

"Have you what?"

"Met a real witch?"

Her lips turn up, and with the flick of her fingers, the dried flower plumps back up, turning into a beautiful, fresh bloom.

"Well then," I say with a nod. "It would seem I have."

"You don't have to look far around here." She puts the blossom in a bowl of water and then returns to the task at hand. "If you're interested in the history of witches here, I recommend hitting up the museum."

"Do you think they have their facts straight?"

Her eyebrows climb at the question, and then she simply says, "I think they did well with what they could understand."

Very well put.

Nera lays at his master's feet and lets out a long sigh before starting to snore.

"He's not usually this relaxed with strangers in the building," Lucy says.

"He's a good boy."

"The best." She reaches down to lovingly stroke the dog's ears, and I suddenly have a vision of her running those hands over *me.*

I clear my throat and offer Lucy a small smile. "I like your shop very much."

The answering smile is immediate and lights up her entire beautiful face.

"Thank you. I do, too. But my favorite place is the garden. Would you like to see it?"

"What if you get a customer?"

"I'll know," she says simply and precedes me through a set of doors that lead through the kitchen of her private residence and out the back door to the garden. Nera follows and runs off to chase after a butterfly. "I come out here every chance I get. If I'm happy or sad, or if I'm scared...this is where I come."

"I can see why," I murmur and feel the power of Lucy's magic pulsing all around me. It's as strong as the pull I have to her. "I didn't know that bluebells grew in New England."

"With the right touch, they do," she says and tickles her fingertips over the blue blossoms. "Ninety-nine percent of what I sell in the shop comes from either this garden or my greenhouse."

"That's impressive."

"I can control the product," she says with a shrug. "I know the plants were grown with the right intention and energy. I don't want any of my customers taking home something sinister or tainted by bad energy."

Her thoughtfulness soothes me.

"I'm sure your customers appreciate that very much."

"It's the right thing to do," she replies and turns to me, propping her hands on her hips as if she's still trying not to reach for me. "Why do I feel like I've met you before last night, Jonas?"

The sound of my name on her tongue is a jolt to my system. It's familiar and surprising all at the same time.

"I don't know."

She narrows her eyes and studies me for a long moment. "I think that was the truth."

"I have no reason to lie to you about that. I don't know why. But I can say that I feel the same. You're... familiar to me."

I step toward her, unable to stay away any longer. Lucy swipes at something on her cheek, leaving a smudge of dirt behind.

Without thinking, I reach up, press my fingertips to her cheek near her ear, and use my thumb to wipe away the dirt.

To my surprise, she leans into my touch, pressing her cheek against my palm, and I feel the shift inside me.

From the look in her green eyes, she feels it, too.

"It can't be," I whisper as she closes her eyes and wraps her hand around my wrist. "It's impossible."

Nera whimpers from his spot at Lucy's knee, and she opens her eyes.

"I have customers."

"And I have to go," I reply but don't pull my hand away quite yet. "I'd like to see you tonight."

Her smile spreads, and I swear the flowers around us open wider in response.

"I'll be around. You'll find me."

And with that, she leads Nera back inside, and I'm left standing in the garden, wondering if what I feel is even possible.

Goddess, I hope so.

CHAPTER THREE
LUCY

"You need selenite wands above the doorframes," Breena says. Her hands are planted on her hips as she looks around Lorelei's beach cottage, making a mental list. "And we'll smudge the whole house before the day is through."

"My mom didn't leave *any* protection crystals," Lorelei murmurs as she pulls a white sheet off the couch in the living room.

"They should be specific to you," I remind her.

"I know that," Lorelei replies. "I'm just surprised she didn't protect or ward the cottage, what with it being empty for a few years now."

"She did," Breena says. "When I saw my mom this morning, she said that Astrid came to take all of her magic away so Lorelei could implement her own. But she did spread some eggshells and rosemary around the perimeter for protection in the meantime."

"I thought you were going to stay here last night," I say to Lorelei.

"No, I stayed at The Merchant," she says, referring to a boutique hotel downtown. "I knew I'd need to clean the place up a bit first, and I didn't know what I was working with. Now, I do. And I'm *so* grateful that you two are here to help."

"It just needs some elbow grease," I say with optimism as I glance around. The cottage is small but has all the modern conveniences. With three bedrooms and two bathrooms, it's the perfect size and sits on enough property that there are no close neighbors. Her view to the east is the ocean, and to the west, nothing but forest. The gardens are lush, overgrown even, and the cottage is secluded.

Lorelei could celebrate the Harvest Moon sky-clad on the shore if she wanted to, and no one would see her.

And knowing my cousin, she just might do that. She's never had a problem with nudity.

"I found a hag stone this morning," Lorelei says with a smile. "I arrived about an hour before you two and took a walk on the shoreline, drawing in the energy of the water and collecting some sand for a spell I'm going to work later. And there it was, as if a faerie had set it there just for me to find."

"Maybe they did," Breena suggests with a smile.

"I think it's a *welcome home* and a sign that you're where you're supposed to be," I add and wander into the kitchen to wipe down the countertops. "I brought you a bunch of herbs and oils, and Breena brought candles and stuff, but we'll have to go buy you some crystals. Do you have any at all?"

"Only a few," she says with a shrug. "I need quite a few things, actually. But given there are only about a dozen metaphysical shops here in town, I'll find it all eventually."

Suddenly, the sound of a bell fills the air, and Lorelei and I hurry back to the master bedroom where Breena is ringing it.

She offers us a shy smile.

"There was just a little pocket of energy here I didn't like. I sent it on its way."

"I thought you said we'd smudge later," I remind her.

"I like sound cleansing, as well," she says. "What are you going to do with all of this space, Lora?"

Lorelei sighs and props her hands on her hips. "Well, in addition to not just dipping my toe back into the Craft but fully diving into the deep end, I'm going to write a book."

"Wow, good for you. What's it about?" Breena asks.

"Salem lore," is Lorelei's response. "And, yes, I know there are plenty of books out there on that subject, but I think I can add my own little twist to things. I've already sold it to a publisher and collected a nice advance."

"Did you hear that, Breen?" I ask and wrap my arm around Lorelei's shoulders. "Our cousin is a fancy author now."

"I haven't written it yet," she says with a laugh and then turns narrowed eyes on me. "Interesting."

"What?"

"It seems our Luciana is holding something back from us."

Breena's gaze turns to mine. "Spill it."

"Have I ever mentioned how much I hate that you're psychic?" I ask Lorelei and then return to the kitchen to get to work cleaning the oven. "And I also hate being referred to by my given name."

"That's why I do it," she says and leans on the doorframe as Breena sits on the countertop that I just cleaned. "Tell us."

"I'm way lost," Breena adds.

"She met a guy," Lorelei says.

"What?" Breena gasps. "We don't keep those kinds of secrets, Luciana—or any secrets."

"Stop calling me that," I say in irritation and then deflate when I see them both smiling at me. "You jerks. Okay, I wasn't going to *keep* it a secret; we were just busy with other things."

"Not busy now," Breena says. "Spill your guts."

So, I tell them about seeing Jonas in the woods and then at my shop.

"Jonas." Breena frowns. "Do we know a Jonas?"

"I don't," Lorelei says. "What does he look like?"

I blow a strand of hair out of my eyes. "Tall. Dark hair. Bright blue eyes. He's...handsome."

"I think that's code for *hot*," Breena says to Lorelei.

"Okay, he's hot." I shrug. "But that's not all the attraction. It's like I'm physically pulled to him. Like if he'd kissed me in that garden, I would have not only let him but maybe jumped him. It's as though I know him. But before last night, I'd never seen him before. And he said he's not from Salem."

"Maybe you were together in your most recent life," Breena suggests.

"Could be," Lorelei agrees.

"Maybe." I purse my lips, thinking it over. "He has magic. Whether he knows it or not, I'm not sure, but the power fairly pulses around him. If he's unaware, I'm not in the market to take on a new witch. I just don't have time. I don't care how hot he is."

"I mean, you've only just met him, and he's not from around here, so it's not like there are wedding bells in the air," Lorelei reminds me. "He said he wants to see you tonight?"

"Yeah. I told him he'd find me around. I like being a little mysterious, especially after I practically wrapped myself around him."

"Stuff like that never happens to me," Breena says thoughtfully. "No soul mate in the coven like Lorelei, no handsome stranger who can't stay away from me. Am I that boring?"

"We know who's meant for you," Lorelei reminds her. "You're just too stubborn to admit it."

"He's never so much as noticed me," Breena says. "Besides, he's boring. I don't want that. I want passion."

"Nothing says a jeweler has to be dull," I point out to her. "Besides, we have to go see him now for Lorelei's crystals."

"What kind of a jeweler has precious stones in his shop *and* crystals for witches?" Breena demands. "I mean, pick one. It's just weird."

"Or, you know...*cool*," Lorelei says. "Come on, this place is as clean as we're going to get it for now, and I want to buy some rocks."

Giles Corey, who happens to be a direct descendant of *the* Giles Corey, the farmer accused of witchcraft in 1692, owns *Gems* on Essex Street, a popular tourist destination. Giles is also a member of our coven through heritage.

His mother is a powerful witch in her own right.

We walk through the front door, and the bell sounds above us. Giles looks up from behind the counter, a loupe against one eye.

"Hi there," he says with a smile. "Welcome home, Lorelei."

"Thanks," she says and picks up a basket to begin filling with her finds. "I need some stuff."

"I have plenty," he says. "I got a new shipment of the most beautiful sunstone towers I've ever seen. I just put them out this morning."

"Do you have some blue lace agate, lapis, moonstone, and selenite?"

"Always the sea witch," Giles says with a grin. "Yeah, I have everything you need. How are you, Breena?"

He turns blue eyes on my cousin, but I see nothing in his gaze besides friendship and kindness.

"Fine, thanks," Breena replies. I can hear the resignation in her voice, and it makes me sad for her. "How have you been?"

"Great." Giles clears his throat. He may be a rock nerd, but he's kind of a sexy one, with messy, dark blond hair and a square jaw. I know she likely doesn't mean for me to, but I notice that Breena swallows hard when Giles replaces his loupe with his black-rimmed glasses.

I browse through the moss agate and choose a few tumbles for myself. It's my favorite. I also choose some black tourmaline and tiger's eye.

My intuition tells me that I need a little extra protection.

The others *ooh* and *ahh* over the amethyst geodes and Giles's stock of super seven. I set my finds on the counter and walk to the window to stare out at Essex Street.

Tourist season is in full swing, with plenty of people milling about. As we get closer to Samhain, the town will swell to bursting, and I won't have time to leave the shop because I'll be packed with customers.

I know that my business thrives because of visitors to our city, but I savor these quiet moments when those of us who call Salem home can fully enjoy it.

By the time we're all done shopping and have left a hefty amount of money in Giles's pocket, it's almost time for dinner.

"Pizza?" Breena suggests.

Before I can agree, I get goose bumps up and down my body, and the same awareness that moved through me earlier today when Jonas walked into my shop settles over me.

"I don't think I can join you," I say slowly. "I'd better head home to Nera."

"And maybe Jonas?" Lorelei asks and smiles knowingly. "Go get 'em, honey. Breena and I will just have to eat all the pizza ourselves."

"I'll see you guys later," I reply and set off for home. It's not far, and I don't mind the walk.

The trees lining the streets are starting to turn color. In just a week or so, it will likely look like everything's on fire with the riot of yellow, orange, and red leaves. This is my favorite time of year.

When I reach the house, I see that my one employee, Delia, has already closed up for the day. She comes in three times a week to take over in the afternoons for me.

I adore her.

Nera rushes over to greet me, and after I rub him down and kiss his head, I reach for my basket to gather flowers in the garden.

Maybe the feeling I had earlier was wrong.

But when I step outside, I see that it wasn't. Jonas is standing at the garden gate, his hands in his pockets, waiting.

When I step outside, his eyes light up, and his lips tip into a half smile.

"You don't have to wait out there," I inform as I walk

toward him, feeling that same pull to him that I did earlier.

"I do, at least until you invite me in," he says.

"Are you a vampire?" I pause in opening the gate, waiting for his reply.

"No. Do you believe in such things?"

"Of course."

"Well, I've never met a vampire, outside of a psychic one, and I'm certainly not one myself. I just believe in manners is all."

I smile at that and then open the gate to invite Jonas in.

"I was about to make dinner," I say, taken aback once again by the pull I feel to him. "You're welcome to join me."

"Thank you. I'd like that."

He pets Nera and follows me into the house.

"Have a seat," I offer, pointing to the barstool at the island. "You can chat with me while I cook."

"I'm at your service," he says. "I can cut and prep, but I'm not a great cook."

"No need. You're a guest. I hope you like fish and chips."

"I don't remember the last time I had them," he admits. "Sounds great."

"Okay, then."

I pull the fish out of the fridge and set the oil on the stove to heat up.

"So, we established earlier today that I'm a witch," I

say as I break an egg and toss the shell into a jar for later, then whisk the white and yolk with a fork. "Now my question is, do you realize that *you're* one, as well?"

I glance up and see Jonas's eyebrow lift. "You think I'm a witch?"

"I know you are, Jonas. The power comes off you in waves."

He sniffs, exhales, and narrows his eyes at me. And then, without looking away from me or moving, lights the candles all around the kitchen, one at a time.

I grin. "I never could master that one."

"How nice it must be to be who you are. Not having to hide your gifts or worry about persecution."

I narrow my eyes at the statement and reach for the flour. "No one is going to burn us at the stake. Not in this lifetime, anyway."

But he doesn't laugh as I intended. His expression is sober as he watches me dredge the fish in the egg mixture and then the flour before sliding it carefully into the oil.

"You said you're not from Salem," I say as I put the fries in my air fryer. "Where *are* you from?"

"Honestly, I'd like to hear more about you," he says. "Tell me more about your Craft and your business."

"Well, that's easy." I smile and flip the fish over. "I was born here in Salem, as were my parents and theirs, going back for as long as recorded history of such things —all witches, of course."

"Were your ancestors killed in the witch trials?"

I still and then look over at him. "Of course, not. No *actual* witches were murdered in those trials, Jonas."

"I know. I was wondering if *you* knew."

I nod and get back to the task at hand. "My dad passed away when I was a kid. He was a fisherman, and his ship went down about ten miles out on the Atlantic, along with my two aunts' husbands, as well."

"That's tragic."

"It was a horrible time," I agree. "I have two cousins, Lorelei and Breena. Each of the three sisters had one child. A girl. The six of us have always been extremely close. Then, my mother passed away last year."

I say the last few words on a whisper.

"I'm sorry, Lucy."

"Me, too."

I look over at him and feel close to tears. I *never* cry, and certainly not in front of sexy strangers.

"I don't usually get this emotional," I admit, brushing the heel of my hand over my cheek to wipe away the tears that managed to fall. "Have you heard of the Salem witch murders?"

His eyes narrow, and he leans in, listening intently. "No."

"Each year, a witch is killed, usually during the Harvest Moon near Samhain. Everyone in my community lives in fear that they could be the one chosen next. A year ago, it was *my* mother."

"You don't work any protection spells against it?" I

see that his hands have tightened into fists, but it's the only sign that he's anything *but* calm.

"Of course, we do," I say and pull the fries out of the air fryer and plate our meals. "Jonas, I've seen a lot of stuff in my life. Hell, a few months ago, I helped send the evilest entity I've ever seen to hell—or wherever things like that go—after the same entity killed me, and I came back from the dead."

Jonas just blinks at me as if he can't believe what I'm saying. I continue.

"Anyway, I've seen a lot, and I've studied the Craft all my life. Our coven is old, deeply rooted here, and is made up of some powerful people. Of course, we cast circles, protection spells, and carry crystals. And yet, it still happens."

Jonas blows out a breath and stares down at the plate I just slid in front of him.

"I'm sorry if I put you off your appetite," I say quietly. "I didn't mean to do that."

"No, I'm just...absorbing," he replies and takes a bite of the fish. "This is delicious."

"Thanks." I fill Nera's bowl with his food and settle next to Jonas to eat my dinner.

"How did you do it? Come back from the dead?" he asks quietly.

I turn my back to him and lift my hair so he can see the tattoo on the back of my neck. It looks like a simple Celtic knot.

"It's a death ward," I inform him and then turn back

to my plate. "I cast a spell that prevents me from dying from any paranormal entity."

"You're joking."

I shake my head and take a bite of fish. "Absolutely not. I don't believe in interfering with the natural order of things, but there's some crazy stuff in Salem, and most of it isn't *normal*. My three cousins and I all have the ink."

"I have a lot of questions," he admits as he eats. "But I won't bombard you with them tonight."

"What is your affinity?" I ask him. "Obviously, as a green witch, I can control nature. And I'm a little psychic. I've always been told that I know more than most. Lorelei is a *very* talented psychic sea witch. She sees just about everything and speaks to those on the other side of the veil."

"And the other cousin?" he asks.

"Breena is a hearth witch. She has no interest in her psychic abilities, although she's a strong clairalient. She smells things all the time that aren't there. Drives her a little batty. So, how about you?"

He takes a deep breath and wipes his mouth with a napkin.

"I'm a healer," he replies slowly. "And I can move through time."

I tilt my head, completely fascinated.

"You can *time travel*?"

"Sort of," he says. "I can also manipulate fire, as you've seen, but at the heart of things, I'm a healer. Your apothecary is beautiful, Lucy. The products you sell are powerful and magical. I hope your customers understand that."

"Some do," I admit with a nod. "Some are just curious. And, honestly, I don't mind selling to either or both because it serves a need."

"So it does," he says with a sigh. "You fascinate me. What's your full name?"

"Are you going to Google me?"

His lips twitch with humor. "No. I'm just curious."

"Luciana Finch," I say at last. "But everyone calls me Lucy."

"Luciana," he whispers, and the sound of it on his lips doesn't bother me in the least. "What a beautiful name for a breathtaking woman."

"And what's your last name, Jonas?"

"Morley," he says.

"That's an old-fashioned puritan name," I say with a grin, and he answers with one of his own.

"I should go," he says and stands from his seat. "Thank you for dinner. And for the conversation."

"It was my pleasure," I reply as I walk him outside and down the sidewalk that leads to my garden gate. Nera follows and waits at my hip as Jonas walks out and turns to wave at me.

When he's in the trees, and I see the lights begin to flicker around him, I look down at Nera and whisper, "Let's go."

We follow behind Jonas, and I watch as he

approaches the bridge and walks over it, beginning to disappear.

I pick up my stride, hurrying behind, and before the light can dissipate, Nera and I are suddenly thrust through what feels like a freezer, only to suddenly reemerge on the edge of a village I've never seen before.

"Oh, my goddess."

I whirl around at the sound of Lucy's voice and hurry back to her, taking her shoulders in my hands as I shake my head.

"Shh."

"What in the *hell* is this place?" she demands as she takes me in, scowling when she sees my clothes. "What are you wearing?"

"Keep your voice down." I glance around to make sure that no one heard her. It's late enough that most everyone is indoors for the evening but not asleep. When I see that no one's around, I take her hand in mine, trying to ignore the jolt of awareness that shoots through me, and whisper, "Follow me. And be quiet."

Without a word, we hurry to my cabin, and I usher Lucy and Nera inside, taking another look around before closing and locking the door behind us.

My cabin is dark and cold, so I wave my hand to light

the fire in the hearth and the lanterns for light, then turn and find Lucy staring at me with wide, green eyes.

"Ouch," she mutters and shakes her hand as if something just bit her. When she glances down and scowls, I close the gap between us to take a look.

A crescent moon is now on her right hand, at the base of her thumb.

"This can't be happening," I whisper.

"You said that before," she says. "*What*? What can't be happening? And just where are we? I live fifty yards from here, and I've never seen this place."

"Not where. *When*."

A frown forms between her eyebrows, and I pace away to set the kettle on the grate above the fire, preparing to make us both some tea.

"I don't understand," she says, walking through my living space. Nera has already curled up by the fire as if he's done it a hundred times before. "What is this place? Is this a reenactment camp for the tourists?"

"No." I clear my throat and offer her a seat. When she finally takes it, I sit across from her, brace my elbows on my knees, and stare at my hands.

"You have the same mark," she says with surprise, reaching over to trace her fingertips over my hand. "Is it a bite?"

"A crescent moon," I reply, my stomach jittering at the feel of her fingers. "A soul mark."

Lucy's eyes narrow, and then she simply says, "You need to talk to me, Jonas."

"First of all, I need you to keep an open mind and know that you're absolutely safe with me."

She just raises an eyebrow, so I blow out a breath and drag my hand down my face.

"I've wanted to talk about this for three hundred and thirty years, and now that I can, I'm not sure where to begin."

"My mom always said the beginning is a good place to start."

"You're right." I stand and pace to my desk, pulling out my journal in case I need to reference any notes, and then take my seat once more. "The witch trials of 1692 were far worse than what history remembers. They murdered more than twenty people. Far more. And although Hallows End was a separate town from Salem, we weren't safe from the wrath of those hell-bent on killing anyone...*different*."

"Hallows End? Is that where I am?"

"Yes. Hallows End in 1692."

She sits back and eyes me warily. "That's impossible."

"I would have thought so, too." I glance around my modest cabin and gesture to the stove, the lanterns. "But as you can see, there are no modern conveniences here. We are held forever in this time, at least until I can break the curse."

"What curse?"

"The curse of the blood moon," I reply and watch as Lucy gasps. "What is it?" I ask in response to her reaction.

"A weird coincidence," she mutters, shaking her head. "My shop is called Blood Moon Apothecary, and I never understood why I had to name it that. I just knew that I did."

"Fascinating," I murmur.

"So, the town is stuck in 1692, but you townspeople can move back and forth from Hallows End and Salem?" she asks.

"No. Only I can. And don't ask me why, because I'm not sure. I'm also the only one here who remembers and knows what happened. Each month with the new moon, time resets one month, and they live through the same twenty-eight days, year after year, century after century."

"You're the only one who knows?"

I nod slowly. "And now, so do you. I don't know how you were able to follow me here. No one, aside from me, has been in or out since 1692."

"Who cursed the village?"

"I did." I lick my lips and feel my stomach jump at the thought of that night so many years ago. "The witch hunters were headed our way, and because so many in this village are witches, I knew that we would all be slaughtered."

"Many. So, not everyone here has magic?"

"No. There are also Christians here. And still others who have no particular faith at all. But the curse was placed on the whole village, not just those with magic."

She nods. "Go on."

"The decision was made to cast the curse, with the

intention of being able to break it once the hysteria was over. We would essentially make Hallows End disappear, along with any knowledge that it ever existed. We should have been caught here for no more than two years."

"Instead, it's been more than three hundred years."

I exhale, relieved at the understanding in her gorgeous eyes. "Yes."

"Jonas." To my horror, tears fill her eyes, but when I reach for her, she shakes her head and stands to walk to the fire, staring down into the flames.

Nera whimpers and sits up so he can lick his mistress's hand. She brushes her fingers over his head and whispers, "All is well."

That she would work to soothe her familiar when she was in turmoil herself says so much about the woman Luciana is. It makes me ache to touch her. Before I can get up to do just that, she turns and pins me with those luminous green eyes, her lashes glistening with moisture.

"This is a far worse punishment for you than death."

I feel my hands flex in and out of fists, and then I simply nod. "There are days that's true, yes."

"I can help you lift the curse," she says. "I told you earlier—there are powerful people in our coven. I *know* that if we put our heads together, we can lift this and set you all free."

"I don't think it'll be that easy."

"I don't think it's going to be easy at all," she agrees but then crosses to me. She kneels before me and takes my hands in hers. "But this has to stop. For all of you.

We'll find a way, but I don't know enough to do it alone."

"Clearly, neither do I or I'd have lifted it centuries ago."

She looks down at our hands, tracing the mark on her skin and then mine.

"What if you weren't meant to?" She turns her gaze back up to meet mine. "And what in the world is a soul mark? Oh, and why do I feel like I *know* you even though I only met you yesterday?"

I take her hand in mine and bring it to my lips, kissing the new mark as I try to gather my thoughts.

"I don't know why you have the crescent moon," I whisper. "I'm as surprised as you are. I've never seen the soul mark on anyone before. From what I've read and was told, it's a physical manifestation of a soul bond. I've had this mark on my hand since I was a child."

"But mine happened only minutes ago. Is it because we're *here*? Why didn't it happen when I met you in my shop?"

"All good questions," I say with a small smile. "Ones I wish I could answer for you. But mark or no mark, it doesn't change the instant pull we felt as soon as we met."

"*Before* we met," she says. "I followed you to that bridge the other night because I *couldn't* do anything else."

"And I couldn't stay away from you today. Leaving you this evening was...well, it was difficult."

"I'm sorry, but I can't live in 1692." She lets out a short laugh. "I need a shower. And electricity. And, you know, things that don't exist here."

"Don't worry. I'm in no position to ask you to live here. None of the people in Hallows End can see you."

"Oh, I'd forgotten about that." She sighs and pulls her hand out of mine so she can push both hands through her hair. "So, this means you're—"

"Three hundred and sixty years old."

She blinks rapidly and then looks me up and down. "You look good for your age, Jonas."

I can't help but laugh at that.

"Were you born here? In Hallows End?"

"No, I was born in Salem."

"What happened to your parents? Your family?"

"They died a very long time ago. They lived in Salem. I lived here."

"Would there be records of your birth? In a census somewhere or something?"

"No. As soon as I cast the curse, our very existence was wiped out of memory."

She scowls and shakes her head slowly. "So, even your family would have forgotten that you existed?"

"That's right." And it was torture being able to go into Salem and see them but having them not recognize me. My mother once passed me on the street without even a second glance.

"Some of the people who live in Salem now, those who have ancestors from that time, may be the descendants of some of the people still living here in Hallows End."

"You have a very busy mind, Luciana."

That makes her smile. "I overthink everything. But that's true, isn't it?"

"It could be, yes."

"Could they be *your* descendants?"

I narrow my eyes on her. "Is that your way of asking if I had children?"

She simply raises an eyebrow.

"No. I never married or had children."

"Thank the goddess." She sits back in relief. "It would really suck if my soul mate was my great-great-great-great-great times about twelve grandfather."

I blink and then let out a laugh. "I hope fate wouldn't do that to us."

I stand and reach for the rag I use to take the kettle off the stove, then get to work fixing our tea.

"I've added protection to this brew," I inform Lucy as I pass her a cup. "I'd like you to drink it."

"Sure." She sips and then looks at me in surprise. "It's good."

"You thought it would be bad?"

"I don't know. This *is* 1692."

I simply sip from my cup and then shake my head. "I can't believe you're here."

"I'm finding it hard to believe, too." She yawns and looks over at my bed. "Can I curl up for just a little while? I won't sleep. I'd just like to lounge."

"You're welcome to anything I have."

She smiles and then stands to walk to the bed. Seeing her curl up and lay her head on my pillow is another jolt.

This amazing, beautiful woman is in my home, lying on my bed.

And if all of this is to be believed, she's *mine.*

"When did you know you had magic in you?" I ask and cross my ankles in front of me, stretched out to enjoy her.

"I was little," she says and turns onto her back to stare at the ceiling. "I always just wanted to be outside in nature. If I was scared, I'd crawl into my mother's hollyhocks, and it was as though they'd fold around me to protect me. The plants, trees, and flowers are my friends. I have a maple tree in my front yard that is very special to me. It's where I offer my finished spells back to the earth, and where I go when I need a boost of energy. What about you? When did you know?"

"I was also a child." When I think back to those times, it feels like it was only a short time ago rather than centuries. "My parents were part of a coven—a secret one, of course. And in the privacy of our own home, we were taught and practiced. I had two sisters, both younger than me."

"Did your parents live to old age, or were they caught?" she asks as she turns back to watch me.

"They died in their eighties. My sisters moved out of Salem. One went to Philadelphia, or so I heard, and the other to New York. I don't know what happened to them after that."

"I could help you find out, if you're ever curious."

I smile softly, longing to curl up with her, but I stay where I am. "Thank you."

"Can you openly be a witch here in Hallows End?" she asks as her eyes drift closed. "Or do you have to hide it?"

"We don't flaunt it," I reply, standing to cover her with a blanket. "But we don't have to practice in secret."

"Good." She sighs sweetly, and I lean over to kiss her forehead. "So sleepy."

"Go to sleep," I whisper in her ear. "I'll be here."

"Just for a minute."

Nera's head comes up, and I nod, letting him know that all is well.

I have some reading to do. I don't know how any of this is possible, nor do I know if I will find any answers in the texts I have here at the cottage.

But I need to try.

This isn't only about me anymore.

"Jonas."

I blink my eyes open and then sit up in surprise when I realize that Lucy and Nera are still here, and the sun is already up.

"I'm sorry," she says. "You were sleeping so well,

though I don't know how, given you're in that hard chair."

I wipe my hands over my face, trying to clear the sleep from my mind.

"I would have let you sleep, but I don't know how to start the fire, and I can't do it with my fingertips."

She offers me an apologetic smile, and I circle my finger, starting the fire.

"Thanks."

"I thought I'd wake up, and you'd have been a dream," I admit with a sigh.

"I'm here. That bed is *very* comfy for being so old. I have no idea what time it is."

"It's still early morning," I reply. "But you and Nera have to go. I don't want you to be seen."

"I know." She gestures to the dog, who's been lying patiently by the fireplace, and he springs to his feet, ready to follow Lucy's commands. "Is there a back way out so we're not seen?"

"We'll follow the tree line," I reply and step out first, gesturing for them to wait so I can look around.

No one is out yet, so we hurry to the trees and walk just inside them to the path leading to the bridge.

Once on the other side, Lucy's gaze travels up and down me, and she smiles. "It's crazy how your clothes change."

"That's how it's always been," I reply with a shrug. "One more thing I can't explain."

Knowing that we're free of any prying eyes here, I

step to her and cup her face in my hands. Her fingers grip my wrists, and she licks her lips in anticipation.

"I don't want you to think I'm being too forward."

"We're in present-day Massachusetts again," she says with a half smile. "It's okay to kiss me."

I don't know that I've ever wanted anything more.

I lean in and gently rest my lips on hers, and for a moment, we simply stay there, soaking in each other's energy.

And then I have to deepen the kiss, to taste her and fill my senses with her. She presses herself against me, surrendering to me so completely and effortlessly it's humbling.

When I pull back, I brush my fingers through her thick, red hair and smile down at her.

"I can't believe you've been right here all this time, and I never found you before this."

"You weren't meant to," she says, echoing her words from last night. "I don't know what the universe has up its sleeve, but it's all happening when it's supposed to. If you'd have found your soul mate a hundred years ago, I would have been really disappointed."

I chuckle and don't bother to mention that she would never have known the difference.

Or, maybe she would have.

"Jonas, I *know* the people here in Salem can help you. I'm asking your permission to tell them what you told me last night."

I frown and rest my forehead against hers. "Can we trust these witches, Lucy?"

"I'd trust them with my life."

"You may be doing just that if you bring them into this."

She licks her lips and nods. "I know. I wouldn't do anything to hurt you or your community. I trust that not only will they do everything they can to help you, but they'll also keep your secret. I know you don't know me that well, but—"

I kiss her again, cutting off her words. I know her to the marrow of my bones. I feel centuries—*lifetimes*—of connection to her.

"I know you," I whisper against her lips. "And I trust you."

"How do I contact you?" she asks with a trembling breath. "Obviously, there wasn't cell service three hundred years ago."

"No." I lick my lips, still tasting her there. "There's a way, but we should be in the safety of your garden."

"Let's go."

CHAPTER FIVE
LUCY

We step inside my garden and close the gate behind us. Nera climbs the steps to the porch and sits, waiting patiently as if he understands that he's not part of this conversation.

"First of all, this spell isn't for everyone," Jonas warns me as he takes my hand, and I turn toward him. "Some consider it quite invasive."

"What do you mean?"

"We'll be able to hear each other's thoughts," he says, raising his eyebrows. "Not only can we speak to each other telepathically, but you'll be able to hear what I'm thinking, dreaming, etcetera."

"And you'll hear mine," I add thoughtfully. Jonas nods slowly, watching me closely. "What if I want to surprise you with something? Or don't want you to know how handsome I think you are because you'll get a big head? Can I block a thought?"

He chuckles at that and squeezes my hand. "No, I think I want in on those thoughts of yours." He sobers. "You can ask me to temporarily close the connection if you need some privacy, and I'll respect your wishes, Luciana. This link is intensely personal."

"Have you done it before?" I ask before I can stop the words from coming out of my mouth.

"No." He reaches up and brushes at something under my eye with his thumb, and his touch sends a shiver through me. "My parents had the link open from the day they took their vows. I learned the spell from them but have never had a need to use it with anyone."

"You know, I'm not usually a jealous woman. I don't know why—"

"It's different," he says, interrupting the apology. "This is different. And there's no need to be sorry for that. I won't ask about your romantic past, Lucy."

"It's kind of boring, to be honest." I grin at him, relieved when he answers with a smile of his own. "Okay, so it'll be a little intense. But it's the only way for me to reach you. I can't text you."

"If you want to close the tether permanently at any time, all you have to do is say so. It will immediately break the spell. Nothing extra needed."

"Good to know." I take a deep breath and let it out slowly. "I'm ready when you are."

"Just repeat after me," he says, keeping his intense gaze pinned to mine.

With harm to none, blessings to all, we cast this spell, this is our call.

Across time and space, our minds become one, tethered together under moon as in sun.

Your thoughts will be mine, my dreams become yours, within arm's reach as on distant shores.

Choices remain, for me and for thee,

As I will it, so mote it be.

Testing, one two three, I say without speaking and watch his face light up with a smile.

It worked, he says.

Good. "You know I'm going to try this out later, right? I'll *call* you."

Jonas laughs and leans in to kiss my cheek and then my forehead. "I look forward to it. What are your plans for the day?"

"I have a lot of work to do. Delia, my part-time helper, is coming in around noon to help me get some new products on the shelves. I have some calls to make. And you? What do you do in 1692?"

"Research," he says. "In fact, I think I'll go to the library in Salem today."

"I'll keep you posted on what I find out with the coven," I reply. "Hopefully, we can meet with them soon."

His brow creases.

What is it? I ask.

I don't want to get my hopes up too high, he replies as

he kisses my forehead once more and then backs away. "Have a good day, Lucy."

"You, too."

I watch him go and then turn to Nera.

"Who would have thought our lives would take this turn, my sweet boy?" I kiss his head and open the back door of the house. "Come on, we have plenty to do."

———

I've never dreamed quite like this before.

I'm standing at the edge of a circle of people, none of whom I recognize. In the center is a fire, and all the people look afraid as they begin chanting along with...me. I'm the one leading them, but the words aren't familiar to me.

On this night, and in this hour, we pull upon the ancient powers.

The blood moon rises to aid our call, to help us forget and safeguard all.

Protect and hide those in peril's way—conceal this town, come what may.

No more will we be known, no longer be seen,

At new moon's touch, a repeat of what's been.

When danger has passed, and we're hunted no more,

May the curse be broken to open new doors.

By the primal power of three times three,

"This is our will, so mote it be," everyone around the fire repeats, and the flames grow high. Thunder claps

around us, and then everything grows completely still. They all look around in confusion as if they don't know why they're standing near the fire.

I just cast the curse of the blood moon.

Suddenly, time shifts. It's ten years later. I don't know how I know, I just do. *I'm walking through Salem, relieved that the witch trials are over and the hysteria has died down. I know, beyond a shadow of a doubt, that my people would be safe now, but I can't figure out how to undo the curse.*

I glance up and almost stop dead in my tracks as a man and woman, my parents, walk toward me. They both look at me, but there's no recognition in their eyes, and they just keep on going as if I'm a stranger.

Because I am.

My heart aches, knowing that the people I love the most don't know who I am, and I'm unbearably frustrated that I don't know how to change what I've done.

Time shifts again. This time, I'm listening as Salem's citizens discuss the Revolutionary War and later still, the Civil War.

I see the passage of time, and with it, the advancement of technology, and again feel the impotent frustration of not knowing how to bring those conveniences to my community.

I reach the modern day and see through Jonas's eyes, him meeting me in my shop. I can feel that he had the same attraction and felt the same pull *that I did.*

When I wake, I sit up and wipe at the tears on my cheeks.

Don't cry for me, my sweet.

His voice is strong in my head. I take a long, deep breath and realize that Nera climbed onto the bed with me sometime during the night to comfort me.

How did you bear it? I ask as I push my face into Nera's fur.

Don't cry, darling. I'm at the gate. May I come in?

I dash from the bed, down the stairs, and out to the backyard, seeing that Jonas is, indeed, waiting at the gate, looking impatient and...wonderful.

"You don't have to ask," I say as I pull open the gate. Jonas tugs me into his arms. "You never have to ask. You're in my head, for the goddess's sake."

He simply picks me up and carries me back inside, but rather than taking me upstairs, he sits on my sofa and cradles me on his lap. Nera paces next to us and finally sits right at Jonas's shoulder, watching us closely.

"He's worried," I whisper into Jonas's neck.

"That makes two of us," he replies and buries his lips in my hair at the top of my head.

"You have no need to worry about *me*." I pull back so I can look him in the eyes. "For fuck's sake, Jonas, what you've lived through is torture."

"I didn't know you'd dream that when I linked us," he says, shaking his head, his voice trembling with guilt. "I would have done whatever was needed to block that from you."

"No, I'm glad you didn't." I take his face in my hands and feel his arms tighten around me. "If anything, this only reinforces how important it is for us to find a way to break this curse. We *will* figure this out."

"I have one request," he says as he pushes my hair off my face.

"What's that?"

"The next time you run out of your house, please put something on."

I glance down and realize that all I'm wearing is a white tank top that's so old you can see through it and a pair of Hello Kitty panties.

"I mean, the important bits are covered."

He raises an eyebrow, and I grin. "Call me old-fashioned," he says. "Also, I'm still a human man, and you tempt me when you're fully clothed, Luciana. Makes it difficult for me to be a gentleman."

A slow smile spreads across my face, and I press a little closer to him. "Is that so? How fascinating."

His mouth latches on to mine, and I bury my hands in his hair, unable to resist him. My breasts ache for his touch, and as though he just *knows*, his hand closes around one, and his teeth scrape over my lower lip.

Goddess, I want you. Even in his thoughts, his voice is rough with need.

But before I can shift and straddle him, we hear voices in the other room.

And then, "Oops."

Instantly, Jonas shifts to block me from view, and I just sigh.

"Hi, Breena," I call out.

"Lorelei's here, too," Breena replies. "Sorry for interrupting, but we brought bagels from Jaho."

"And I know you need us," Lorelei says, having no issue at all walking right in and propping her hands on her hips. "Hi. I'm Lorelei. And this is Breena. We're all practically sisters. There's something fishy about you."

"*Lora*," I hiss, but Jonas just chuckles.

"It's okay," he says. "It's a pleasure to meet you. I've heard much about you."

"I don't think we've heard enough about *you*," Breena says kindly. "But I'll share my bagel with you, and we can ask all the nosy questions."

"I'm going to get dressed," I announce and climb off Jonas's lap. I walk unashamedly up the steps to my bedroom without even bothering to try and cover myself.

"I like your panties," Lorelei calls after me.

It doesn't take me long to dress in a green sweater and faded blue jeans. When I return downstairs, I find everyone in the kitchen, eating and laughing.

"It's good to see that you're all friends now," I say as I take the extended plate from Breena and bite into a bagel with cream cheese. "Jaho is the *best*. But I'm psychic enough to know that you didn't just come over for breakfast."

"As I said, I knew you needed us," Lorelei says, still

eyeing Jonas speculatively. "I heard you crying this morning over the sound of the shoreline."

"I'm okay," I reply and then roll my eyes when Lorelei frowns at me. "I really am. I just had some interesting dreams, that's all. We've all been dreaming lately."

"Hmm," she replies and pops the last of her bagel into her mouth. "If you say so."

"I do. Also, we need to call an emergency meeting with the coven."

"Why?" they ask in unison.

"Because there's a *lot* going on, and I need their help." I sigh and glance at Jonas.

You can tell them.

I know, but then I'll have to explain it all again with the others. I'd like to tell it just once.

"Why do I get the feeling they're having an entire conversation without us?" Breena asks Lorelei.

"Because they are," Lorelei answers. "And it's rude."

"Just trust me," I plead quietly. "We *need* this meeting. As soon as possible."

"So, he *is* a witch, then," Breena says with a smile.

"You have no idea."

"Thank you all for coming so quickly."

It's only been about six hours, but we're all assembled at the aunts' house, outside on their beautiful patio, sipping tea.

Xander, the coven leader, leans against the pergola post, watching Lorelei openly. His jaw is tight, and a muscle in his cheek ticks in frustration.

But Lorelei just ignores him and sips her tea.

"What's going on, darling girl?" Astrid asks kindly. "And, please, introduce us to your handsome guest."

"Everybody, this is Jonas Morley," I begin and nod when both Astrid and Hilda look at me in surprise. "This is the man I told you about the other day, the one I saw in the woods."

Jonas and I spend the next hour explaining everything to the twenty people gathered. Xander's dark eyes narrow, and he crosses his arms, but he's quiet as he seems to take it all in.

When we finish, there are a few moments of silence as everyone processes the story we just told.

"This is at once amazing *and* horrifying," Astrid says, finally breaking the silence. "Jonas, what you must have witnessed over the past few centuries is just incredible."

"And sad," I murmur. "There has to be a way for us to break the curse. We have the person who cast it here with us, but I'd like to hear Xander's thoughts."

"I have heard of Hallows End," Xander says, and I feel Jonas tense beside me.

"That's impossible," Jonas replies. "The curse itself wiped it from existence."

"There is mention of it in ancient texts," Xander continues, frowning. "I don't know if it's because it was mentioned in a Book of Shadows that it ended up safe from being completely erased, but the lore states that it's located in Europe. Not here in New England."

"It's fifty yards from my back door," I say, my tone as dry as the Sahara. "I've seen it."

"And everyone in Hallows End is caught in a time loop," Margaret Sanders says thoughtfully. "That's interesting to me."

"It was done on purpose," Jonas replies. "Because although we all agreed that it was the only way to protect us all from persecution, we are also human. The fear that someone would try to leave Hallows End to see their family was great, so we included the time loop—and the memory loss—on purpose."

"When the curse is broken," Percy McGuire asks, "will they remember? And will they immediately age and die? Or will they just continue forward as if only a month has passed?"

My head whirls to Jonas, and my jaw drops. "I hadn't even thought of that."

Jonas grips my hand, and not one person in attendance *doesn't* notice, though they don't say anything.

"I don't know," Jonas admits. "You need to understand, I never intended for the curse to last this long. It was supposed to be just a couple of years, at most. I suspect that once it's lifted, the citizens of Hallows End will simply go on to live their lives. However, they won't remember. Only I will know everything."

"Gods, they'll be thrust right into the twenty-first century," Giles says, speaking for the first time.

"What's the alternative?" Xander asks. "We leave them there for eternity?"

"That's not what I'm suggesting," Giles says, shaking his head. "It's just...the people they love will be gone. I can't imagine what that would feel like, and—"

"It's unthinkable," Jonas adds with a nod. "Because it *is* unthinkable. I understand that none of this is your responsibility. If you are unable or unwilling to help, I completely understand. I don't know what's kept us in Hallows End all of these years. I *do* know that each time I try to lift the curse, something blocks me. I don't know what entity might be trying to stop me and wanting to keep us in Hallows End in 1692. If you *are* willing to consider the possibility of helping, however, I can't express to you how grateful I am."

"When did the mark appear on your hand?" Xander asks, surprising us all.

"What mark?" Hilda demands, and I hold up my hand for all to see.

"It appeared when I reached the other side of that bridge and entered Hallows End."

Without a word, and with his eyes on Xander, Jonas lifts his hand.

"Soul marks," Astrid whispers.

We hear a door slam inside the house, and I smile at my cousins.

"Seems my mother has something to say about that."

"Oh, your mother has had *plenty* to say this whole

time," Lorelei says. "But I'm not allowed to share it with you. Not yet, anyway."

For the first time, Lorelei looks Xander in the eyes and addresses him.

"We have to do this, Xander. We have to do whatever we can to lift the curse of the blood moon. Because it's no longer stuck in the past."

"No, it's not," Xander agrees with a sigh full of confusion and questions. "It impacts us all. There is work to be done. It's up to each of you how much you want to be involved."

"I think it's safe to say," Percy says slowly, his old, lined face solemn, "that if there's anything any of us can do, you'll have it from us. How many of us have ancestors stuck there?"

"There's no way to know that, given things were wiped from public record," I say softly. "But whether they're linked to us by blood, religion, or simply because they're *people*, I think we should do whatever we can to help."

"Agreed," Hilda says.

Everyone nods in agreement, and when I look at Jonas, I can see that he's overwhelmed by gratitude.

I told you.

He looks down at me, emotion swimming in those amazing blue eyes.

I didn't want to hope. This could change everything.

"Lucy, may I have a word?" Xander asks.

"Sure." I stand and cross to him as Astrid and Hilda approach Jonas. "Thank you, Xander."

"I want you to be careful," he says and braces my shoulders in his hands. "I want extra protection spells on you at all times."

"Me?" I frown up at him. Xander is *tall*, towering at almost seven feet with hair and eyes so dark they're almost black. He's an imposing, intimidating man who can devastate or heal. He can be terrifying or the most comforting person I know. "I'm not the one in danger."

"I'm not yet convinced of that," he says, shaking his head.

"What do you see?" I demand and reach for his big hand.

"I don't see *anything*." His voice is full of passion and worry. "And that's what scares me."

"You're never scared."

He slowly shakes his head again and then swallows hard.

"Not often," he admits. "Something about this just doesn't feel right."

"I'll stay with her," Jonas says, and we both turn in surprise. I didn't sense him approaching.

"I'm not sure that's the answer," Xander says. "You're a stranger here, and I can sense how great your power is. How do I know *you're* not the danger we need to be wary of?"

Jonas nods and brushes his hand over his mouth in frustration. "I understand your point. I would rather die than risk any of you. I know that I only have my word, but I assure you, I'd *never* harm Lucy. Or any of you."

Xander doesn't answer. He simply nods once and then walks away, seeking out Lorelei, who scowls when he approaches her.

"Do they know they're meant for each other?"

"Oh, yeah. And she fights it like crazy."

CHAPTER SIX

He's waited centuries. Watched. Hunted. Killed. But it always lacked the fulfillment he craved.

But now, they're both marked, and it has begun. It's time.

CHAPTER SEVEN
JONAS

I've combed through these texts dozens of times over the years, hoping I missed something before that might help. Inevitably, I end up sucked down rabbit holes, and this time is no different.

I'm so deep into the history of the goddess Lilith that when a knock sounds on my door at just past two in the morning, I jump and then cross quickly to open it.

"Lucy," I say in surprise, pulling her and Nera inside before looking around outside to make sure no one saw them. "What are you doing here?"

I turn to find her green eyes wide, her skin pale. She's shivering in her thin green dressing gown.

"I didn't know if I could get here without you," she says through chattering teeth. I reach for her and pull her into my arms as I stoke the flames in the fireplace higher, filling the room with more warmth. "I didn't know if it would work."

"Hey, it's okay," I soothe, running my hands up and down her lean back as she burrows against my chest. "Why didn't you call for me? I would have come to you."

"I did." She pulls back and licks her lips. "I did call for you. And I hit what felt like a wall."

I narrow my eyes on her, and my heartbeat quickens. She needed me, and I couldn't hear her? That is absolutely unacceptable. "I was reading, sucked into it pretty deep, but I should have heard you. I'm so sorry, Lucy. Come. Let's warm you up, and you can tell me what happened."

I lead her to the chair by the fire and cradle her against me as Nera lies next to us.

"What happened? Was it nightmares?"

"I was wide-awake, I know that much for sure," she says and fiddles with the button on my shirt, her fingers not quite still. "Jonas, I don't spook easily. As I told you before, I've seen some scary things in my life, especially in the last year or so. But what happened tonight ranks up there in the top three."

"Tell me."

"I was walking through Salem."

"At this time of night?" I tip up her chin so I can look into her eyes. "At this time of *year*?"

Salem is not as safe as it once was, I say telepathically.

"It's not unusual," she insists. "If I can't sleep, which is often the case, Nera and I will take a walk. I know the spirits roam at night, but they don't bother me. Most aren't intelligent, just residual hauntings and echoes of energy."

"So you're not afraid of ghosts, then."

"No. Definitely, not. It was a lovely night, and I thought I would just walk to the shore and back. Nera was calm and happy with the idea, so we set off. I don't walk at night alone."

"Good."

The thought of her being unprotected, especially now that I know something or someone is out there killing witches every year, doesn't sit well with me.

"We were on our way back home, maybe two blocks from the house, and the hair on the back of my neck suddenly stood up. Nera stopped walking and moved right in front of me as if guarding me or protecting me from something."

I glance down at the hound, whose gaze hasn't left his mistress.

"The air grew so cold, Jonas. Not windy, just suddenly *freezing*. I called out to you in my mind, but I couldn't reach you, and Nera started to growl. Snarl. I've never heard him do that before. And then a red dog walked out of the bushes, but I'm telling you right now that it wasn't really a dog. I don't know how I know that, but I'm telling you, while it looked like a dog, it had human eyes."

I frown down at her, and she shakes her head.

"I know it sounds crazy."

"I didn't say that."

She swallows hard, and tears fill her emerald eyes. "I don't know what it was, why it happened, but it was terrifying, Jonas."

I pull her to me once more and hold her close, tucking her head under my chin.

"You're safe, my darling. You're safe right here. What happened next?"

She clears her throat and pushes her face against my shirt. I can feel the fear radiating out of her, and it's killing me.

"What happened, Lucy?"

"It wrinkled its nose at me, and then it just walked away. It didn't look back at us; it just left. Nera stood still and watched until it was out of sight, and then he told me we had to hurry home. Once we got there, I didn't go in, I just kept going into the woods because I *needed* to get to you."

"Do you often wear your dressing gown when you go for walks at night?"

She looks up at me in surprise and then scowls. "You're going to criticize my *outfit* at a time like this?"

"No." I drag my fingertips down her cheek. I can't stop touching her. I've never felt a connection like this to anyone in my life. The very *need* to touch, connect, and simply *be* with her.

She's the part of my soul I didn't know was missing.

"What was it, Jonas?"

"Likely a skinwalker."

She blinks at me and then shivers. "I thought those

were only horrible stories that people made up to scare each other."

My fingers dance over the tattoo on the back of her neck, and she closes her eyes.

"You said it yourself. You got this death ward to protect you from the paranormal things that happen in Salem. That town has always been full of activity, even before the English settled there and dating back to the indigenous tribes that moved through."

"I know," she whispers. "And it's always been something I embraced. I mean, I protect myself, but I've never been afraid. Maybe I'm more on edge because of everything we have going on and because we don't know how it'll end. But this was so far out of the *normal* part of Salem's paranormal that it sent me into a complete panic attack and...I just needed you."

"I'm glad you came here," I reply softly and kiss her forehead. "But I hate that you were frightened."

"I'm starting to feel better," she replies. "You can turn down the fire a bit."

With a wave of my hand, the fire dies to a soft flame, just enough to keep the chill out of the air.

"I thought you might come to *me* tonight," she admits with a half smile.

"I'd planned to," I reply and brush her gorgeous red hair behind her ear. "I got sucked into reading, and it completely consumed me. I didn't realize just how much until you knocked and pulled me out of my trance. I wish I had come to you earlier."

"We're together now," she says, and her gaze falls to my lips. "I have a confession."

"You can tell me anything."

She licks her lips, and then she lifts her eyes to mine. "I've been attracted to men before. I'm not entirely innocent."

My eyes narrow. "Is that supposed to make me feel good?"

"I'm not done." She presses a fingertip to my lips, and I feel it all the way to long-dormant places. "I'm not innocent, but I've *never* had a physical reaction to anyone the way I do to you."

"What does it feel like?" I whisper and allow my hands to roam over her lightly, gently following the contours of the gorgeous hills and valleys of her curvy body.

"It's a burning need," she says softly. "A wonderful and powerful yearning to be touched and to touch in return. And it feels like the only thing that will help is *you*. I know our minds are linked, and the urge to be near you is powerful, but I also want to touch you constantly. It's as if I just can't keep my hands to myself. Before this, I wouldn't have considered myself an overly touchy-feely woman."

"I'm glad I'm not alone in that." I drag a fingertip down the bridge of her narrow nose. "You have an open invitation to touch me whenever you'd like, Luciana."

She tips her lips in a soft smile before pressing them to mine. Just as it was before, I'm swept up in lust so thick and all-consuming that all I can do is breathe her in and surrender. Her heartbeat is strong under the palm of my hand as I cup her breast and tease the already tight nipple. And when she shifts in my lap and straddles me, I'm certain I'll go mad from wanting her.

She opens her gown and lets it fall down her arms to the floor, then crosses her arms and lifts her shirt over her head, exposing her naked torso. The firelight dances over her skin, casting her in a glow so magnificent that I swallow hard.

"You're the most beautiful woman I've ever seen," I breathe, leaning forward to taste her.

Lucy's fingers dive into my hair to hold me to her, and her hips move instinctually, pushing against my hardness.

But suddenly, Nera begins to bark, pulling us out of our haze.

"Nera," Lucy hisses as she slides off my lap and tugs her gown around her. "Stop that."

But he doesn't. He jumps at the door and snarls until Lucy places her hand on his back.

"He's terrified," she whispers, turning her frightened green eyes to meet mine. "What is going on?"

"I don't know." My voice is grim as I shake my head. "You two back up. Nothing can hurt you here. I'll take a look around. Perhaps it's a deer or something."

"Deer can get in and out? I mean...of the boundary?" she asks.

"Yes. Just another piece of this that's confusing. Sit tight."

I open the door slowly and peek my head out, but the night is still. I don't sense anything in the darkness.

But Nera doesn't overreact. So, I walk outside, close the door behind me, and reach out with my mind.

Nothing and no one is about. The townspeople are all tucked safely in their homes.

But when I walk a few houses down from mine, I see Alistair coming out of his house.

"Oh, Jonas," he says with a sigh, closing his eyes. "You startled me. I could have sworn I heard a dog barking nearby. I was just going out to investigate."

"I thought so, too," I reply and shake my head. "But there's nothing out here. Perhaps it was a little thunder."

The other man looks up to the sky. "It *has* been awfully stormy lately. You could be right. Well, have a good night, then."

He returns to his home, and I breathe a sigh of relief that he didn't press for more as I return to my cabin.

"There's nothing out there," I say as I walk inside. Lucy has redressed and is sitting with Nera by the fire. "Perhaps Nera is just on edge because of what happened earlier."

"Maybe," she says, but I can see by the look on her face that she doesn't think so. "Also, that's the second time we've been interrupted."

I cup her face and brush my thumb over her cheek.

"It's been more than three hundred years, Lucy. What's a few more hours or days?"

Her eyes widen. "Wait. You haven't had sex in *three hundred years*?"

"Three hundred and thirty years, six months, and a few days, but who's counting, right?"

She blinks and then tips her head back and laughs. "I have so many questions. I thought people waited until they were married in 1692."

"I don't believe that witches have ever subscribed to that way of thinking," I reply with a smile.

"I don't think I want to know the answers to the rest," she says thoughtfully. The smile is still in place, but she shakes her head with certainty. "Definitely, not."

"Anyone I once had a physical relationship with has been dead for centuries," I reply and then raise an eyebrow. "Can you say the same?"

"So, they didn't live here, then? You haven't had an affair with someone spanning over three centuries?"

I slowly shake my head. "No."

"Well, that helps the jealousy factor. Which is another new thing for me, by the way. And before you ask, the answer is no. I have no one else in my life."

"Of course, you don't. You're too loyal. You wouldn't be here with me if you were in love with someone else."

"I don't even know *why* I feel jealous," she continues, not meeting my eyes as she pets Nera's head. "I mean, it's

not as though we're in some kind of exclusive relationship or anything."

"Look at me." My voice is hard, and the look in her
eyes is surprised as she turns to mine. "We may not have
said the words, but I think it's clear that this is, without a
doubt, an *exclusive* relationship. You don't feel *jealous,*
you feel territorial. And I can confirm that I feel the same
way. If a man put his hands on you, I'd have to kill him."

She blinks. "I don't think that was just a figure of
speech."

"No. It was not. You say that this is new for you, well,
it is new for me, as well. But I am not willing to share you
with anyone. So, now that we have established that, we
can move forward without any feelings of uncertainty."

"I just realized that your speech is quite modern, at
least for the most part. But when you get angry or
worked up, it becomes more formal. Similar, I assume, to
how people spoke in the Puritan days."

With that small storm over, I reach for Lucy and pull
her to her feet.

"We should go. You really shouldn't be here.
Someone was coming this way to check out the barking
he thought he heard."

"I'm sorry."

"No." I step into her and kiss her forehead. "There's
no need to apologize. You needed me. But it's risky
coming here. From now on, I'll stay with you at night."

"Won't people realize you're gone?"

"Probably not. I can move in and out so I still have a

presence here, but I won't leave you alone at night again."

"Thank you." She simply wraps her arms around me and holds on tightly before pulling back and gesturing to Nera. "I assume we leave the same way as last time? In the trees?"

"Yes." I put the fire out, extinguish the candles, and take the few books I've been reading through. "Let's go."

"I've been doing a lot of reading," Xander says. He invited me to his home, and I decided to come today while Lucy is working in her shop.

From the moment I met him, I knew that Xander was a powerful witch, perhaps more so than anyone I've ever come across before.

I hope I can pick his brain.

"That makes two of us," I reply and set my books on the table.

"I found mention of the curse of the blood moon," he says and holds up his hand. A few seconds later, a book floats across the room from a bookcase and lands in his outstretched palm.

I simply blink.

"This is my seven-times-great-grandmother's Book of Shadows," he says and gently opens the front cover.

One I recognize.

"I've studied it before, but it has been more than a

decade. And at that time, the curse wasn't something I was looking for."

"Of course. May I ask her name?"

"My seven-times-great-grandmother?"

"Yes."

"Katrina Harwood."

I still. "Are you certain?"

Xander frowns and raises an eyebrow. "Of course, I'm certain. Did you know her?"

I stand and walk to the wall of windows that look out onto Chestnut Street.

"Her home was on this property," I say quietly. "The street looked much different then, with small cabins and dirt roads for the carriages, but Katrina lived here."

"I know," Xander says behind me. "How did you know her?"

"She was my sister." I turn back to him and take a deep breath. "I'd heard that she moved to New York with her husband, Thomas."

"She did, for a while. They were worried about being persecuted for the Craft and stayed away for about ten years. But when her parents grew older, they came back to Salem with their family."

"Did they have children?" I ask, hanging on his every word, then realize what I said. "They must have. Because...here you are."

"Six," he confirms. "Four died of childhood diseases, but two lived well into old age."

"And the Craft lived on through her children and grandchildren."

"Yes," he confirms. "Jonas, there is no mention of you *anywhere.*"

"Of course, not." And it's a sharp stab to the heart to be reminded of it. "I told you, any existence of Hallows End and its people were erased from existence."

For the first time, I see compassion in the other man's eyes.

"I can feel the love you had for her," he says.

"She was...one of a kind. So smart. Dedicated. She and Charlotte, my other sister, were extremely gifted in the Craft. Very powerful witches."

Xander's eyes light at the mention of Charlotte's name, as if the more I speak, the more he believes me.

"They were co-leaders of their coven," he confirms.

"Charlotte went to Philadelphia."

"No." He shakes his head. "That was the rumor they told to the townspeople so she wouldn't be hunted and persecuted. She just went to Boston for a few years and then eventually came back here."

"With Charles? Her husband?"

"Charles died of measles," Xander says. "You never looked into all of this, even though you could move between worlds?"

I shake my head and drag my hand down my face in frustration. "The temptation to see them would have been too great, and they didn't know me. It was too painful. And a bit of cowardice. The curse was never supposed to last this long, as I told you. I thought I'd be reunited with them after only a short time. And when it became obvious that it wasn't going to happen, I had to cut the emotional ties as well as the physical because watching them all age and die and having them not know me was its own form of punishment."

"Yes. I imagine it would be." He sighs and looks down at the book. "I can tell you about their children and grandchildren, if you ever want to know about them."

"Thank you. Perhaps once this is all over, we can have that conversation." I return to the chair across from him and sit. "In the meantime, I'm sitting across from my seven-times-great-nephew."

Xander's eyes fill with humor. "Yes, you are. My mother and grandmother are both still living. They're in Florida now, but I'm sure they'd like to meet you."

"When this is all over," I repeat. "I'd like to meet them, too. For now, I'd like to focus on lifting this curse, Xander."

"Of course." He turns his attention back to Katrina's Book of Shadows. "She mentions the curse in here but states plainly that those of the Craft were always warned against using it because it was so unpredictable. She says, and I quote, 'Hallows End could be lost forever.'"

"She knew what my plan was," I say slowly. "So, she must have written that before I cast the spell. She warned me against it, but I didn't think there was any other way."

"We're going to figure this out," he assures me. "We're going to harness the power of the Harvest Moon at the end of the month. It falls *on* Samhain this year."

"Will we be ready?"

"We have no choice," he says simply.

"Xander, I have a question."

He raises a brow.

"I feel the power in you. Just what is the extent of your magic?"

His lips turn up, and then, right before my eyes, he becomes a black cat.

I stand and back up, not sure I believe what I just saw.

"You're kidding."

"*Meow.*" He licks his paw and then becomes human once more.

"I've never seen that before."

"Our bloodline has only grown more powerful through the ages," he says with a satisfied grin. "Sit, and I'll tell you more."

CHAPTER EIGHT
LUCY

Lorelei beat me to Breena's house today. The three of us decided to gather and start getting some special things ready for our Samhain celebrations.

"I've missed doing this together," I inform them as I walk inside and take my raincoat off, hanging it by the door before shucking my boots. I take a long, deep breath. Breena's house always smells of baked goods and whatever incense she's been burning. It's comforting—like walking into a big hug. And her home is the epitome of *cottagecore*, with homemade quilts thrown over the backs of her couch and chairs and other crafts she's done herself set about. She has the fire burning and her cauldron set above it, bubbling away.

"You were gone too long, Lora."

"I know," she says with a heavy sigh as she sits back on the couch, her legs pulled up under her. "But it was good for me. I missed this, too. Samhain is my favorite holiday. And, of course, I love being with the two of you. I was *so* homesick."

"You could have come home at any time," Breena reminds her as she stirs something into three mugs. "You're *always* welcome here."

"I know. I know I am. I just...*couldn't*. I needed the time away to do a little soul searching. As I said before, I didn't do much with the Craft while I was gone, but I did a *ton* of meditation, some chakra work, and spoke a lot with my guides and ancestors."

"Here. I made hot cider with apples that I found at the farmer's market," Breena says, passing me a mug of steaming cider before handing one to Lorelei. It smells of cinnamon and apples and makes me smile.

"I love fall." I sip the brew and sigh in happiness. Then, the ivy I sent home with Breena catches my eye. It's sitting on her mantel, along with some half-burned candles, dried flowers, spell bowls, and photos of us as young girls. I walk to it, whisper, and watch as it comes back to life. "Really, all you have to do is water this thing, Breena. It's thirsty."

"I think I overwater it in fear that I'm not watering it enough," she admits. "I'm good at a great many things, but keeping plants alive has never been one of them. Anyway, what did the ancestors tell you, Lorelei?"

Our cousin sips from her mug thoughtfully, and then tears begin to fill her eyes. Both Breena and I rush to her in a panic.

"Oh, geez, I didn't mean to make you cry," Breena says, rubbing circles on Lorelei's back.

"Were the ancestors mean to you?" I ask, and when Lorelei lets out a watery chuckle, I breathe a little sigh of relief.

"No." She brushes away the tears. "It's just...I *know* that leaving was the right decision at the time. I just couldn't stay in Salem after everything that went down with Xander."

"That's perfectly reasonable," I agree and brush at her pretty auburn hair.

"But every time—and I do mean *every* time—I meditated and spoke to my guides, they said the same thing. *Go home.* They told me to face what was happening here rather than running from it." She looks into her cider. "I don't like feeling like a coward."

"Honey, you are *not* a coward," Breena insists and kisses Lorelei's cheek. "Not in this or any other lifetime. Self-preservation is important, and that's what you needed to do. We're just grateful you're here now."

"As long as you've healed," I qualify. "Because if you only came back because of the dreams but don't feel strong enough to be here, that's not okay."

"I know. And that's not what this is." Lorelei takes a tissue from Breena and blows her nose. "I'm much stronger now than when I left. And I *want* to be home. I enjoyed my work and my time on the west coast, but this is where I'm meant to be."

"You *are* much stronger," I agree. "And you held

your own the other day at the coven meeting with Xander."

"That man makes me so fucking mad sometimes." Lorelei shakes her head. "Yet, at the same time, I want to climb him like a tree. It takes everything in me not to touch him. It's really annoying."

"Xander's always been alluring," Breena admits. "He's a charismatic, magical, potent man. I mean, it's like he got all the hot genes in the world."

"You're not helping," Lorelei says, her voice dry. The three of us crack up. "But you're also not wrong. Yes, he's beautiful. There's no other way to describe him. And the sex is just out of this world, but it's more than that. It's the connection I've felt to him since we were children. I've known, for my *entire* life, that I would be mated with Xander. But now that's not to be, and it's been really difficult to deal with."

"Maybe it *will* still happen—"

"It won't," she says, interrupting my thoughts. "It's never going to happen. So, I'll work with him when I have to. Aside from that, I'll stay the hell out of his way. I have my cottage, a book to write, and a centuries-old curse to lift—which is going into said book, by the way. I don't need Xander."

"Okay, so, let's get to work," Breena suggests, changing the subject with a bright smile. She's always been the peacekeeper, the easygoing one—the one who wants everyone to be happy at all costs.

Even if that means jeopardizing her own happiness.

"Lucy, did you bring the herbs?"

"I did," I reply and set my bag on the table. We're making special Samhain incense out of various herbs and spices that will be perfect for burning during our ritual. "I brought some extra sage, orange peel, and star anise for you guys, in case you need it in any of your workings."

"Thanks," Lorelei says and takes the small bags gratefully. "And I brought some stuff to make some extra protection spell jars. My guides and intuition tell me we'll need all the protection we can get over the next month."

"Awesome. I have plenty of black wax to seal them all with." Breena grins. "This will be fun. Oh, and before I forget, I have gifts for the two of you, too."

She hurries out of her living room in excitement.

"She's always so gifty," I say, and Lorelei smiles in agreement as Breena returns, holding orange gift bags with black tissue paper. "It's so festive."

Breena just grins and watches as we open our gifts, and then all I can do is stare at the white cloth in my hands.

"*Breena*," Lorelei breathes, sharing my awe. "This is *gorgeous*."

"They're ancestor altar cloths," Breena explains as I run my fingertips over the embroidered names of our family members, lovingly sewn into the fabric. My name is in the middle, and then the names branch out around mine. People I love and admire. People I miss so much. "With it being Samhain and the veil being so thin, it's always good to focus our altars on our ancestors, but you can really use these any time of the year. Or not at all, if you don't like them."

"How could anyone *not* like this?" I ask and then cross to pull her in for a hug. "It's absolutely beautiful. Please, tell me that you made one for yourself, as well."

"Of course, I did. It's already on my altar. I changed it out for the season, and it's all ready to go for All Hallows' Eve."

"You'd change it out in July if you could," Lorelei says with a smile.

"Hey, some people leave their Christmas trees up all year." Breena shrugs. "I'm no different when it comes to Samhain. Okay, let's start on the incense."

But before we can get started, the broom by the front door falls with a loud *thwack.*

We jump and frown at it. We always leave a broom by the front door, upside down, to keep the evil spirits at bay.

"Company's coming," Lorelei mutters as Breena stands to pick up the broom. Before she can do it, the front door flies open, and wind whips through the cottage, snuffing all the candles.

Immediately, the three of us join hands and begin to chant.

You are not welcome here. You've not been invited.
Take your leave; all evil has been smited.
Nothing that does not serve us may stay.
Only love, joy, and light come through the doorway.

Our power builds as we chant the simple spell over and over again until the wind dies, and the door slams closed once more.

With our hands still clasped, we look at each other, unnerved.

"Like you said, Breen," Lorelei says at last, "the veil is thin, and this is Salem. Shit's about to start happening, and we're always targeted because of our magic."

"You're right," I agree and feel the tattoo on my neck pulse, ready to defend against any attack. "And we have our wards."

"I say we make the protection jars first," Breena suggests. "I also have pendants that we can make into tiny protection jars to wear at all times."

"I stopped at Giles's store and bought extra tourmaline," Lorelei says. "We'll spell them and keep them on us, as well."

"I'll make some for Jonas, too," I murmur, thinking of the man I'm quickly falling in love with. "He should have the added protection, given that he moves between worlds."

"Agreed." Breena nods once and then walks to the door to pick up the broom, setting it back in place. "Let's get started."

The three of us worked well into the evening. When I got home, Nera wasn't entirely happy with me. But the two of us are settled in now, having eaten dinner and taken care of business outside in the rain.

I know that Jonas will come to me tonight. He's been here every night since my and Nera's horrifying experience during our walk. He spends most days in Hallows End, but without fail, he comes to me.

Though despite being so attracted to him I can hardly see straight, we haven't made love.

By the time we fall into bed each night, we're exhausted, and I know that we both have a lot on our minds. Not to mention, something always inevitably interrupts us.

But tonight is *the* night. I've given Nera a stern talking to, and he knows to leave us be for the night unless there's an emergency.

I've just changed into a sheer, nude nightgown and pulled on the flowy green robe when I feel Jonas cross the bridge.

My body breaks out in goose bumps, and every nerve ending in me awakens.

With an excited little dance, I run for the back door, down the steps, and through the garden. When I meet up with Jonas in the woods, I launch myself into his arms and kiss him like my life depends on it.

His hands grip my butt as my arms and legs wrap

around him, and he continues to walk to my house as he ravages my mouth.

"I want you," I whisper against his lips. Jonas grins, gets me through the back door, and then pins me against it when it's closed. It drives me *wild*.

"It's going to be fast," he says, apology hanging in his voice.

"Good." I moan when he reaches down between us and fingers me, making sure I'm wet and ready for him.

And then he's inside me, his blue eyes locked on mine, driving himself deep and thrusting hard before emptying himself into me. He shudders, his face buried against my neck as he lifts me once more and carries me up to my bedroom.

"Now, we go slow."

I lift an eyebrow as he gingerly lays me on my bed. I lost my robe somewhere on the journey up here. I lean back on my elbows, dressed only in the sheer nightgown as Jonas strips out of his blue Henley and jeans and joins me on the bed.

"Wow," is all I can say as I drink him in. I've touched him before, but I had no idea just how lean and muscled his body is.

His lips twitch into a satisfied grin.

"If we're interrupted this time, I might perform murder," he says, his eyes every bit as greedy as I feel.

"No interruptions," I assure him and let my fingertips trail over his defined biceps and up to his shoulders. "Just you and me. All night."

"I've wanted to give you time," he admits softly and then frowns. My candles suddenly light all around the room.

"Too dark?"

"I want you in candlelight," he says and presses a kiss to my cheek. "As I was saying, I wanted to give you time. Our relationship is new."

"And yet I feel as though I've known you forever. I'm more comfortable with you than I've ever been with anyone else. I don't need any more time, Jonas."

"Thank the gods and goddesses." He grins and then lowers his head to kiss around my breasts. His hands roam over me, gently in some places and more eagerly in others, but every bit of it is absolute ecstasy. "Now that a few centuries of pent-up energy is gone, I can take my time with you, learn every line. Every curve. And listen to you moan."

"I had no idea you'd be a dirty-talker."

He stops, and his gaze whips to mine, then he grins and starts chuckling as he lays me flat on my back and pins my hands above my head with one hand.

He didn't exaggerate. The pace is slow and easy, but my heart pounds in my chest as his mouth and hand roam over me. He whispers words of appreciation, and when he's so far south he can't reach my hands anymore, he lifts his head and sternly says, "Keep them there."

"Okay."

I expect him to use his mouth on me. Instead, he kisses and licks his way down my legs. He kisses the arches of my feet, each toe, and when I can't take it anymore and reach for him, Jonas simply shakes his head.

"Hands. Above. Your head."

I bite my lip and comply, and I'm rewarded when he spreads my legs wide.

His chest heaves as he takes a long, deep breath, and then, with his eyes pinned to mine, he finally lowers his head and presses his lips to my clit.

"Jonas!" My hips buck, and his hands cradle them as he takes his time licking and exploring all of me. Finally, when I'm reduced to a whimpering, shivering mess, he crawls over me, kisses his way up my body, and with his hands planted in my hair, and those eyes glued to mine once more, he pushes inside of me.

The candle flames grow around us, and it's unlike anything I've ever felt before.

You're amazing, he says in my mind and tips his head down so he can kiss my neck. *You feel incredible. You're everything I've ever wanted and didn't know I needed, Luciana.*

I can't believe you were there all this time.

I feel him smile against my skin, and then his mouth is on mine, nibbling my bottom lip.

I raise my hips to meet him and pull my legs back and higher on his hips.

"Lucy," he whispers, and I can feel that he's close now. "Ah, baby."

With my hands planted on his ass, urging him faster and deeper, he comes apart and succumbs to his orgasm.

Much later, after we've cleaned up and are curled up together in bed, he pulls me against him and kisses my forehead.

"I'm pretty sure the earth moved," I say. "Literally. Was there an earthquake?"

"Maybe a small one."

When I look up into his face, he's grinning with so much pride it makes me giggle.

Suddenly, Nera starts to bark downstairs.

"You've got to be kidding me, Nera," I mutter as I get out of bed and pull my robe around me. "I told him not to bug us unless it was an emergency."

"We should bring him up here," Jonas suggests. "He's not used to being without you."

"Sometimes a girl needs some privacy," I remind him with a wink and then walk out of the bedroom and downstairs to where Nera is standing, looking into the apothecary and snarling. "What is it?"

He doesn't even look back at me, he just continues barking and growling, the hair on his back standing on end.

"Nera?"

But he only gets louder. I call out to Jonas. *Help!*

I hear his footsteps above me as he hurries from the bed and down the stairs. When he reaches us, he walks directly in front of us and starts to speak.

"You hold no power here." His voice is strong and firm. "You are not welcome. Get out of this house and don't return."

Nera whimpers and leans into my side, and I gently pet his back from his neck to his tail in long, reassuring strokes.

A quick wind passes through, and then everything goes quiet once more.

"I have wards." I hear the shakiness in my voice. "I place spells and jars all over this building. How in the world was something able to get in?"

"It's strong," is all Jonas says, his face set in grim lines. "And first thing tomorrow, we're calling the coven to come and set protection spells around not only this house but Breena's and Lorelei's, as well. I felt what happened at Breena's today."

"Oh." I blink, surprised. "I didn't even connect this to that."

"It's the same." He props his hands on his hips. He's still shirtless, and his jeans hang low on his lean hips.

I could just bite him.

"I don't know why it's attempting to get to each of you now. Unless it's trying to scare you away and keep you from helping *me.*"

But *I* know why. Damn it, I should have realized earlier today what it was.

"Jonas. It has to be the same entity that killed my mother. The one that's killed them all."

"In that case, we'll do more than cast spells. And we won't wait for morning."

CHAPTER NINE
JONAS

"It's almost dawn," Lucy murmurs. Nera hasn't left her side all night as we traveled as a coven from house to house, starting at Lucy's and then going to Lorelei's. Now, we're at Breena's.

I was impressed by how quickly the members of the coven came together. How they jumped into action, bringing their tools with them so we could work as a team to add layers of protection to each of the homes.

We've just finished a mirror spell, completing the night's work. The rest of the coven members have taken their leave, looking weary and on edge as they head home to ward their own homes, just in case.

So far, only the three cousins have been under any kind of attack, but there are still several weeks to go until Samhain, and anything could happen.

After saying goodbye to the last members to leave, Xander joins me, the cousins, and Giles, who stayed back. Giles's face is set in grim lines, and his hands are on his hips.

He looks good and royally *mad.*

"Why do I feel like we haven't done enough?" he demands, looking at Xander.

"We cast the circles," Xander reminds Giles, not defensive at all but sounding as though he completely understands where the other man is coming from.

We're all frustrated.

"I'm not so sure salt—even black salt—eggshells, and a little tourmaline will put this...whatever it is, off. You know as well as I do that these women are talented, experienced witches. Their homes weren't unguarded to begin with."

"I understand," Xander says with a nod. "And I feel the same."

"We're all worried," I add. "And it's not just eggshells and crystals. We've just built the power of more than twenty magical beings into the wards of each of the houses. They'll hold."

"I don't like the ladies being alone," Giles admits with a sigh. "And I don't mean for that to sound chauvinistic." He glances at the women. "Of course, you're capable of protecting yourselves, but there's strength in numbers."

"He's not wrong," Lucy says. "There *is* strength in numbers, but I honestly think Jonas is right. What we all did tonight was powerful and will keep us safe."

"Agreed," Lorelei hurries to add. "My cottage is safe. I'm fine."

Xander's eyes narrow, and it looks like he wants to say something but just clenches his jaw and fists his hands at his sides.

The push and pull between the two is fascinating to watch.

"I can stay with you," Giles offers to Breena, much to her apparent surprise. "It's not a problem for me at all. I'm sure you have a guest room. You'll hardly know I'm here."

I notice how Lucy and Lorelei share a surprised look, and Lorelei winks.

"You don't have to stay," Breena tells him with kindness and goodness dripping from every word. "Thank you for coming to help tonight, we really appreciate it, but I'm fine. And if I need anything, I know I can ask for help."

"I can't leave yet," Giles replies, shaking his head stubbornly. He removes his glasses and rubs at his eyes as if trying to get rid of a horrible headache before replacing them. "It's almost as if it's physically impossible for me to go. The right thing is for me to stay and protect you."

"I honestly don't need your protection," Breena replies, her voice firmer now.

Lorelei rolls her eyes, and Lucy is already shaking her head.

Don't say it. Do not say it. The thought comes fast, but before Lucy can say it out loud, Lorelei speaks.

"Oh, come on, Breena. You've had a crush on the man for your *entire* adult life. You know you want him to stay."

"Shit," Lucy whispers next to me.

Giles's face sobers, and he frowns over at Breena. "What?"

Breena closes her eyes, her face flushed with embarrassment, and Lorelei covers her face.

"I'm sorry. I have no damn filter, and I'm punchy from no sleep."

"What?" Giles asks again, but Breena only shakes her head and forces a smile for the man.

"Thanks again for your help." Her voice shakes. "Have a lovely day."

And with that, she hurries inside and closes the door behind her, turning out all the lights. The five of us are left staring at each other.

"*Lorelei,*" Lucy says. "What in the actual fuck?"

"I'm sorry," Lorelei whines.

"What?" Giles says once more. "Breena's interested in *me*?"

"Come on," I say gently and lay my hand on the other man's shoulder. "I'm new here, and even *I* can see it."

His mouth opens and then closes, and once more, he takes off his glasses to press his fingers into his eyes.

"I didn't mean to do that." Lorelei's voice is full of misery. "Honest, I didn't."

"It's time he knows," Xander says to her softly, but I notice he doesn't reach out to touch or reassure her.

"Why?" Lucy asks, and the anger in her tone actually surprises me. "Why is it time that anyone *told* him and not let them figure it out organically? Just because the two of you have known that you're fated since you were in fucking diapers, doesn't mean that everyone else is on the same path. It was rude and hurtful, Lorelei. And you *know* how soft Breena's heart is."

"I know," Lorelei replies miserably. "I'll go apologize right now."

"No, I'll go," Giles says, holding up a hand.

"*None* of you will go," I interrupt, and all heads turn to me. "She's embarrassed, and it will only make things worse. Leave her be for now—to recover a bit. Giles, if you go in now, she'll think it's only because you feel obligated."

"I *do*," he says.

"That's not what she needs from you," I reply. "I think we're all tired here. We should get some rest."

"I'll take you home," Xander offers to Lorelei, but the woman shakes her head.

"I'm fine."

"If you think I'll let you go anywhere alone until after the end of the month, you've lost your gorgeous mind," Xander replies, his voice perfectly cordial.

Lorelei's green eyes sharpen in temper.

"If you'll *let* me?" she demands. "In case you missed it, I'm a grown-ass woman who does what I want, when I want, and I don't consult you for any of it. You made damn sure of that, Xander Appleton. And I'm in the kind of mood this morning that I almost *dare* anything to try to fuck with me. I'd take delight in tearing something apart."

With that, she sets off, her cloak billowing behind her like the pissed-off witch she is.

Lucy simply smiles at Xander. "For someone so smart, you're *really* quite dumb."

His eyes narrow, and then he shifts into a raven and flies off, I suspect to keep an eye on the woman he loves.

"Don't overthink it," Lucy advises as she turns to Giles, who's staring at Breena's cottage, his hands planted on his hips and his face lined with misery.

"You obviously don't know me very well if you think I won't." He shakes his head. "I'm going to stay here in my car for a while. Just to make sure she's safe."

"That's a little creepy," Lucy says, making Giles smile. "Sweet, with a tinge of stalker."

"I won't stay too long," he promises and walks to his car, settling in the driver's seat and seeming to brood.

"Do you know how to drive?" Lucy asks as she, Nera, and I make our way to her vehicle.

"No. I don't go much farther than a couple of miles from Hallows End, so there's never been a need."

"Do you want to learn?"

"Someday," I reply as we all climb in, and Lucy starts the vehicle, driving us to her house. "Your aunts invited me to their home for dinner tomorrow evening. I'm to come alone."

"It's not as ominous as it sounds," Lucy rushes to assure me. "It's just that they want you all to themselves so the cousins can't take over the conversation."

She glances my way as she turns into the driveway and smiles.

"You don't have to promise to marry me or anything."

I can't do that until we lift the curse and I'm able to promise to spend the rest of my life with her.

My stomach clenches at the thought of watching her grow old without me. Of watching her die while I'm stuck in this hell for more centuries to come.

"That's not going to happen," she says softly, and rather than getting out of the car, she reaches over to take my hand.

"We don't know that," I reply, and after giving her hand a squeeze, I get out of the car and walk around to open her door for her. Nera joins us as we walk wearily up the steps to her door, worn out both physically and spiritually from the night's events. "We should try to catch a few hours of sleep."

"You don't have to go to Hallows End?"

I shake my head and take her hand as I lead them both up to the bedroom. "No. No one is expecting me for anything. Let's rest."

Nera immediately lies on his bed, and once Lucy and I shed our clothes, we climb into her bed together.

But rather than settling in for sleep, she turns to me and presses her lips to my ear.

"I need you," she breathes.

And, without any more words, we make love in the silence.

Lucy's aunts live in a beautiful little stone cottage in the woods, not far from the ocean. With ivy and roses climbing the side of the building, and the established gardens, not much has changed here in the past few hundred years.

This used to be my good friend Samuel's home. It didn't look all that different back then.

The house was obviously sturdily built.

Before I can knock on the door, it opens, and both Astrid and Hilda smile out at me.

"Welcome," Hilda says kindly. "We're so happy you could join us."

"Thank you for the invitation," I reply and, upon their gesture, walk into the cottage. To my surprise, another woman is standing in the living room.

She looks just like Lucy.

"I'm sorry, we haven't met."

The two aunts share a look, and then Astrid lays her hand on my shoulder. "I didn't realize you were a medium, Jonas."

I frown down at her and then look back at the third woman, who's now smiling at me. "I'm not."

"Fascinating," Hilda says. "Well, that's Agatha, Lucy's late mother. And I'd say that it's because of her intense love for her daughter and her curiosity about *you* that she's showing herself to you."

"She doesn't look like a ghost to me."

All three of them laugh, and I'm surprised by just how human Agatha looks. I certainly can't see through her. She's as real as I am.

"Come." Astrid gestures for me to follow them into the kitchen, where the table is already set for dinner. "I hope you like lobster rolls and coleslaw."

"I can't say I've ever tried it, so this is a day of new things." I smile as I sit in the chair. Before long, our plates are full, and we're talking as though we're old friends.

Agatha also sits at the table, watching me with shrewd green eyes.

"You all have the same eyes," I say without thinking. "All six of you. It must be a strong family trait."

"All the daughters throughout the centuries have them," Astrid confirms. "It's a piece of our magic."

"They're beautiful."

"You're so charming," Hilda replies with a coy smile. "And I can see why you've taken a shine to our Luciana. She's quite lovely and smart. Her business is flourishing, and with no magical help from us."

"No, she wouldn't need the help of magic for that," I agree. "I was struck by how wonderful her shop was the first time I went in. I'm a healer, and I hadn't seen the likes of the tinctures and salves she has in a very long time. It was refreshing."

Agatha smiles, almost beaming with pride as the aunts nod in agreement.

"I use her carrot eye cream," Astrid says. "I don't love the smell, but I think it's really helped the crow's feet."

"Jonas." Hilda kindly changes the subject from skincare. "How are you holding up?"

"I beg your pardon?"

"You've been through so much," she continues. Breena is so much like her mother—her voice and mannerisms are Hilda's. "I suspect it might have broken a weaker man. How are you *really*?"

I sip the tea they served with dinner, thinking it over. They'll know and call me on it if I give them the standard: *I'm just fine, thanks for asking.*

As they should.

"I can honestly say that this is the first time in more than three hundred years that I have hope." I turn to Agatha. "And that's because of your daughter and her friends and family, who have so selflessly and graciously offered to help me."

"Is it also because you're in love with our niece?" Astrid asks.

"Without a doubt," I agree, not even thinking to hide the fact that I'm irrevocably in love with Lucy. "She is...*everything*."

"And if we can't lift the curse?" Astrid demands, her

voice strong but not rising. "What will you do then, Jonas?"

"Return to Hallows End without her." The words leave a rancid taste on my tongue. "I will always do what's best for her. But it's my greatest hope that we *can* lift the curse and that I can be with Lucy."

"How sweet," Hilda says and glances at Agatha, whose eyes are now narrowed. "May I ask if you were born here and who your parents were?"

"Of course." I tell them, and when I say my parents' names, their faces turn ashen, and they share a glance. "What is it?"

"Xander's ancestors," Hilda says.

"Yes. He and I discovered that just the other day. It's fascinating. Of course, he told me that any mention of my name was not there."

"They lived next door to this very house," Astrid continues, and I nod.

"I remember. Of course, the building is long gone. How did you know that?"

"We've made it our business to know everything about the witch lineage in this area," Hilda replies. "We're historians of a sort."

"Nosy," Astrid adds with a wink. "We're just nosy, really. Well, that's fascinating. I'm sure Xander was surprised."

"We both were."

"You must protect my daughter." Agatha speaks for the first time, startling us all.

"You can speak." I blink in surprise. She hadn't uttered a word before this.

"Danger is coming," she continues. "And unless your love for her is pure and true, you won't be able to help her. She will be lost, trapped between worlds."

I frown in confusion. "I don't understand."

"You must stand with her. You will be afraid. You will want to step back, but it's imperative that you don't."

"Agatha." Astrid's voice is hard. "That's enough."

"He has to know," Agatha insists, but Astrid shakes her head.

"It's their path to take, sister. Enough."

Agatha's eyes are full of worry as she stands from the table. "Protect my daughter." It's the last thing she says before leaving the room.

"No matter which side of the veil you're on," Hilda says softly, "you're still a mother. She's afraid for you both. We can't see what the outcome will be, but if you're true to each other, and if you work together, you have a fighting chance."

"Great." I push my empty plate away. "A *chance*."

"That's all we ever have," Astrid points out. "Now, let's get to the fun part of this interrogation. What makes you think you're good enough for our niece?"

I blink at her and then chuckle. "I'm likely not. But according to the marks on our hands, and the way I feel when I'm with her, I'd say she's stuck with me—if she'll have me."

"And where do you see yourself living in five years?" Hilda asks, surprising me. "Will you try to take her out of Salem?"

"I've been here for almost four hundred years. Why would I leave now?"

"Perhaps you want to see more of the world," Astrid points out. "It's a big world out there, and it's easy to travel it now."

"But our community, our home, is here," I reply honestly. "Might we travel? Perhaps. But unless it's *her* wish to move away, I'm happy here. I would be thrilled to simply be set free of the curse and able to live every day with Lucy, right here in Salem, for about fifty years. Growing old is a privilege. One I would like to experience with her."

"Watch yourself," Astrid says, a smile tickling her lips. "I might try to snatch you up for myself."

"Get in line," Hilda agrees, and I can't help but laugh with them. "I'm so very happy that you found our girl. She deserves someone who values her."

"Do you have other family in the area?" I ask, changing the subject. "Or is it just the six of you now?"

"We have extended family all over the country, but most of them think we're a little nutty." Astrid shrugs. "Others are also witches and members of covens in their own communities. When Lucy went through her ordeal in New Orleans several months ago, many of those cousins went to help."

I narrow my eyes on her. "Her ordeal?"

"Well, it sounds like that's something the two of you need to talk about," Hilda says brightly. "Would you like some strawberry shortcake? I picked the berries from my own garden."

"This late in the season?" Astrid asks.

"I froze them," Hilda clarifies.

I want to ask for more details about New Orleans, but I can see the subject is closed for now.

"I'd love some, thank you."

———

"So, what happened?" Lucy asks when I return to her house after dinner.

"You didn't listen in?" I pull her to me for a quick kiss.

"I felt like it would have been rude," she admits. "But I'm *dying* to hear about it. Were they overbearing with their questions?"

"Not at all." I kiss her hand and lead her to the sofa, pulling her into my lap the way I've become accustomed to. "They're wonderful women. I also met your mother."

She sits up straighter and frowns down at me. "What?"

"She was there, as plainly as you're here. I thought they'd invited someone else to dinner at first before they clarified who she was. You look a lot like her."

"*You* got to see her?" Lucy slumps a bit with sadness.

"No matter how hard I try, I'm never able to see or hear her."

"Are you jealous?"

"Of course, I am."

"Well, don't be. You'll see her. We all have the ability. We just have to practice."

"Did she speak to you?"

"Hmm." I don't know if I should tell Lucy what her mother said. She's had many scary things happen lately, and I don't want to add more fear to her plate. "She smiled a lot. I think she just wanted to check me out."

"Probably." She rests her head on my chest. "What did you have to eat?"

"Something called a lobster roll."

"Oh, those are my favorites."

"It was delicious." I brush my fingers through her hair. "Luciana."

"Yeah?" She tips her face up to look at me. "What is it?"

"We need to talk about New Orleans."

She wrinkles her nose and then sighs.

"Okay."

CHAPTER TEN
LUCY

"How did you learn that they needed help in New Orleans?" Jonas asks after I've told him the whole story about how I helped some friends hunt a killer earlier this year. His face remained impassive as he listened to the craziness of what we went through, but his hands fisted when I told him the part about being kidnapped.

"Through a friend," I reply. "Their coven needed our help, so I went."

"But your cousins didn't go?"

"Lorelei was teaching in California, and I knew, given the situation, that Breena shouldn't go. Not because I think she's weak, because she's one of the strongest people I know, but if anything catastrophic happened, I needed her here with the aunts."

Jonas's eyes narrow.

I rush on. "Hundreds of people from all over the country came to help. Not just me. And it took every single one of us to finish it. It was terrifying and fascinating all at once."

"And something I hope you don't do often."

I smile at him and reach for his hand. "No, I think vanquishing evil once in my life is enough. Although I have a feeling New Orleans won't be the last time I'm faced with something sinister."

Nera yawns on the floor at my feet, then turns on his side to continue sleeping.

"Did you know about New Orleans in 1692?"

He lifts an eyebrow. "I don't believe many European settlers were in that area until the early 1700s. So, at the time of the witch trials, probably not."

"*Probably not*? You don't remember?"

"It was a long time ago," he reminds me. "And without any kind of communication systems like telephones or telegraphs or such things, no. We likely wouldn't have known about explorations happening in the rest of the country until long after it was done."

"So, how do you know about all of it now?"

"I've had a lot of time on my hands and access to a library through the years. I listened. I read."

"The more I think about it, the more I realize just how bazaar the world will be to the people of Hallows End when they're set free. I don't know how they'll deal with it."

"I think the first priority is actually setting them free. Then we can worry about the mental health of the people. They will need help, Lucy."

"They'll get it."

"You speak as though it's a foregone conclusion that we'll succeed in lifting the curse."

"Of course, we will. Didn't you hear the story before? I've vanquished evil and come back from the dead. I can handle a measly *curse*."

Jonas laughs and takes my hand, lifting it to his lips. "I'd like to take you to bed."

I yawn and stretch my arms over my head. "Yeah, I'm pretty tired. Sleep sounds good."

His lips twitch. "Sure, you may sleep. Eventually."

"**D**o we have more dandelion root?" Delia asks as she walks back to the kitchen, looking a little frazzled.

"I have some in the oven now. It'll be ready in a couple of hours. Who needs it?"

"Mr. Edison," she replies. "He's constipated again. I'll tell him to come back in the morning."

"You can let him know I'll drop some by later. I'm going to Breena's anyway. Are you almost ready to close up for the day?" I ask.

"Yep. Mr. Edison is the last customer."

"Okay. Don't worry about doing the floors or anything. I have more stocking to do, so I'll be puttering around for a while. You can just head out when you're finished with him."

"Are you sure?" Delia frowns at me. "I don't mind staying to help."

"I know, but I *also* know that you have a date tonight, and you'd much rather go primp for that."

Her pretty lavender eyes widen in surprise. "How did you know that? Actually, don't answer that stupid question. You always know everything."

I laugh and shoo her off. "Go, enjoy your date."

"Okay, I'll see you soon."

Delia blows me a kiss and walks away with a spring in her step, off to deliver my message to Mr. Edison and then close up the shop for the day.

Today's been the first day in a while that things felt somewhat normal. Jonas headed for Hallows End first thing, and Nera and I tended the garden and then got right to work. I've spent the day with customers, stocking shelves, drying herbs, and mixing potions and salves.

It's my favorite way to spend the day, and it feels wonderful to be in my happy place.

"Bye, Lucy!" Delia calls out before I hear the door close and lock behind her.

It was *such* a good idea to hire Delia. We've been so busy this year, and October has set a new record for sales for the shop.

Goddess bless the tourists.

By this time next month, the crowds will disperse and head back home, and Salem will quiet down once more. If this year has been any indication, I'll need more help before spring.

That doesn't hurt my feelings in the least.

"Come on, buddy, let's go fill some jars."

Nera follows me out to the shop, and I gather the big jars from the herb wall that I need to refill. St. John's wort, thistle, basil, and chamomile are completely empty, so I grab those jars first.

The newly dried herbs are laid out on parchment-paper-lined baking sheets, and it makes such a satisfying sound when I tip the paper and the herbs slide off into the jar.

Thirty minutes later, all the jars are refilled, and I make a note of the others that could use a refresh tomorrow before I move to the oils and salves.

My skincare line has become a new favorite among the customers and needs to be restocked badly, so I make a list of what I need to gather from the supply closet, then check the homemade incense and smudging sticks.

"Delia was busy today," I say to Nera. "She went through a lot of stock."

The hair on the back of my neck suddenly stands up, and I turn to check behind me, making sure no one is watching me through the door.

That sometimes happens shortly after closing, when customers are hopeful that we're still open.

But no one's there.

"Hmm." I snag a smudging stick for myself. "I know we usually do this just once a week," I say to Nera as I light the end of the bundle of rosemary, black sage, and pine for protection. It's wrapped in rose petals to make it pretty and invite love into the space. "But we've had more people in and out than usual, and who knows what kind of icky energy they've brought with them? You know the drill."

Nera takes his place at my side, and starting at the doorway, we make our way widdershins around the room, spreading the smoke from the bundle and moving from left to right in a circle as I cast the protection spell.

"Any energy here that does not serve me must go. Only love, joy, peace, and comfort may stay."

We systematically make our way through the whole house, not just the shop, and I open windows as I go to let any banished energy leave the building.

When we return to the apothecary, I snuff the bundle.

"As I will it, so mote it be."

I smile down at Nera before getting back to work.

"There, that feels better already, doesn't it? It's just that so many people are in and out of here so often. We have to clean out that energy. Let's recharge the tourmaline while we're at it."

I gather my crystals from the top of the doorframe and the corners of the room and take them back to the kitchen with me, placing them in a selenite bowl for cleansing, and then get to work restocking the shelves in the shop.

On one of my passes through the kitchen, I stop to check the eye cream I have cooking in the Crock-Pot.

"Almost done. Perfect timing."

I swear something passes by the front door when I walk out to place the bottles and tubs on the shelves.

A shadow.

But Nera hasn't uttered any kind of noise at all, and he's usually *very* in tune with anything supernatural.

"I've been awake for too long," I mutter. It only takes me another hour to get everything looking just the way I like it and then sweep and mop the floor.

Nera smiles up at me when I stow the mop.

"That's right, we're all done for the day. We get to go see Breena now."

His head cocks to the side.

"That's right. Do you want to go see Breena?"

His whole body starts to wag in delight, making me laugh.

"I think that means yes. Okay, let me grab my bag, and we can walk over."

But lightning fills the sky, then thunder booms just before the rain starts hammering down.

"Never mind, we'll drive."

I grab the dandelion root for Mr. Edison and the bag of goodies for Breena and then we're off, rushing out to the safety of the car.

"We only ran for ten yards, and we're both soaked," I

say with a laugh as I start the engine and drive the half mile or so to Mr. Edison's house. Once I make that delivery, I take us to Breena's.

I haven't seen her since the other morning after our night with the coven.

If Breena hasn't reached out to one of us in *days*, it's a clear sign that she's mad.

"Come on, let's go make this right."

Nera and I hurry through the downpour to Breena's covered porch, and I press the doorbell.

A few minutes later, my cousin opens the door.

"Oh, I wasn't expecting company."

"I brought you some things, and I wanted to talk to you."

Breena's too polite to turn us away, so she just shrugs and gestures for us to come inside.

"The weather sure decided to get dramatic," she says as she closes the door behind us, then leads us to her craft room, where she has all kinds of things covering her worktable. "I'm just making moon wreaths for my online store."

"These are always gorgeous," I murmur as I pick up one of the finished products and admire the craftsmanship. It's a crescent moon wrapped in flowers and branches and adorned with crystals. "You should make a few for me to sell at my place."

"Oh, that would be nice. Do you think your customers would be interested?"

"Are you kidding? Of course, they would. And I need more rose quartz candles, too."

"I have it on my list to make some tomorrow."

"Perfect, thanks. Listen, Breena—"

"I'm fine," she interrupts, but when her green eyes meet mine, I can see that she's *not* fine.

She just doesn't want to talk about it.

"Have you spoken with Lorelei?"

"No." She won't look up at me, just concentrates on securing an amethyst to the moon as if it's heart surgery. "She called, but I didn't pick up."

"No one meant to hurt you the other day."

"I'm not hurt." Her smile is fake, and it makes my heart ache like a sick tooth. "As I said, I'm fine."

"*Breena.*"

"Okay, I'm embarrassed." She shrugs and then sets the moon down when her fingers fumble. "Is that what you want to hear? That I felt humiliated and sad and just wanted the earth to open up and swallow me whole? Because I did."

"I know." I reach for her, but she moves out of my reach. "But I also know, without a doubt, that Lorelei didn't mean to blurt it out like that. We were all emotional and exhausted and—"

"I get it," she says, interrupting me again. "I do. Lorelei wouldn't purposely hurt me. But she did say it in front of Giles, and it really hurt my feelings that she wasn't more thoughtful. Because I would *never* have done something like that to her."

"I know," I repeat. "You have such a sweet heart, Breena."

"Do you know what's exhausting?" All traces of sweetness and forced happiness are gone from her face now. There's no more pretending here, and I'm so relieved because Breena has a habit of covering up what she's feeling to make others comfortable.

"Tell me."

"Knowing that I'd walk through fire for people who wouldn't walk across the street for me."

"Breena—"

But she holds up her hand, and I stop speaking, ready to hear her out.

"I *know* that you both love me. I'm not wallowing so deeply that I don't recognize that. And I also know that you'd both do anything for me. But in that moment, in just *that* instant, Lorelei was careless with me, and her love for me and my feelings was nowhere to be seen. And that, Lucy, is exhausting for me because I *always* have others in the forefront of my mind."

I simply cross to her and wrap my arms around her because I don't know what to say. She isn't wrong. As much as Lorelei loves Breena, she *was* careless in that moment, and it was wrong.

"I'm sorry, Breen," I say softly. "I know that Lorelei is miserable, too."

"Did you speak with her?"

"No, I can just feel it. From both of you."

She sniffles and then pulls back so she can reach for

one of her pretty little vintage handkerchiefs. This one is sage green with little pink rosebuds on it.

It's *so* Breena.

"Has anything else happened since the other day?" I ask her. "Supernaturally, that is."

"No, and thank the goddess for it because I simply don't have time to deal with an entity throwing a temper tantrum. My shop suddenly blew up with orders."

"Well, that's great! What can I do to help?"

"I'll need more herbs and flowers." She wipes at her nose once more. "I heard through the grapevine in one of my witchy groups on social media that the hashtag *witch101* just took off on that clock app, so now there are all kinds of people wanting to dabble a bit in the Craft."

"That's both exciting and...scary."

"Yeah. I took down any products from my site for hexing. We don't need the newbies hexing everyone who's ever crossed them."

"Good idea."

"I'm also restocking all the protection spell bottles and crystal sets because they'll need that."

"I love you."

She looks at me in surprise, her eyes blinking. "I love you, too. What is it?"

"I just absolutely *love* that unlike some witches who think they need to keep all the secrets for themselves, you're ready to jump in and help. That you're worried about someone hurting themselves."

"Well, people are way more powerful than they realize, and they need *someone* to help them. I might start an account on the clock app and make tutorial videos for easy spells and stuff. Maybe no one will watch it, and I'm sure some people will roll their eyes at me, but it could be good."

"I love it."

"Will you guest star sometimes?"

I grin, warming up to the idea. "Sure. We can film in the shop, and I'll get some free advertising out of it."

"Hey, great idea," Breena says, beaming. "Do you have *your* online shop open yet?"

"I need to hire more help for that," I admit. "Because I don't want it to cut into my time in the garden."

"Get on it," she advises. "You're missing out on a lot of money by not offering things online. Do you know how many people from all over the *world* would place orders just so they could say they bought it from a witch in Salem?"

I smirk but then stop to give it some thought.

"You know, you're not wrong."

"I'm absolutely right. Mark my words, before long, we're going to have to go in on a warehouse space so we have more room to make our stuff."

The thought makes my arms break out in hives. "I don't want to do that. I *like* making everything myself in my little kitchen."

"You won't be able to keep up with it there for long. You'll need more ovens, more sink space, another stove. That house is gorgeous, but it's not big enough for that."

"Well, damn it. Maybe I don't need to expand. I make enough money for what I need."

Breena giggles and then reaches for my hand. "You could be the only person I know who doesn't get excited at the thought of raking in more money."

"I don't *need* more money."

"Exactly." Her phone rings, and when she looks down at it, she scowls and sends it to voicemail.

"Who was that?"

"Giles," she says, shaking her head. "He won't stop calling. My phone rings three times a day, like clockwork."

"Maybe you should do something *really* crazy and answer it."

Breena licks her lips and sets the phone down. "No. I don't know what to say, Lucy."

"Well, he clearly has something to say to you, so you could just listen to him."

Before she can reply, there's a knock on the door. Nera's head comes up, but he doesn't whimper.

"I'm just popular today," Breena says as she opens the door, stopping short when she sees it's Giles. "Uh, hello."

"Hi. I wanted to come talk to you."

"I'm busy," she replies, her voice stronger than I've ever heard it. "I'm sorry, I'll have to see you another time."

"Are you sure?" he asks.

"Yes. I'm not ready to talk to you."

"You won't invite me in?"

"No," she says, shaking her head. "Have a good day, Giles."

And with that, she closes the door and turns to me.

"First, I want to say good for you for sticking up for yourself," I begin. "But also, who are you, and what have you done with my cousin?"

CHAPTER ELEVEN
JONAS

I find it harder and harder to go back to Hallows End each day. Not because of the modern conveniences in Salem or even the perpetually dreary weather in my village.

It's because leaving Lucy gets increasingly more difficult.

I fear that leaving her will be permanent one day— and that makes my heart bleed.

But I have people to see to and a home to take care of in Hallows End. So, each day, I return. I left Lucy and Nera still sleeping peacefully this morning as I left well before dawn. I know she will likely have a busy day in her apothecary as Salem grows fuller and fuller of people every day.

And it will only continue to do so as we get closer to Samhain.

As I walk, I think of the books I need to trade out,

and that I want to start keeping my Book of Shadows in Salem.

I don't know why I feel that it'll be safer there, but something in my mind demands it be so.

And I'm not one to go against my guides.

As I cross the bridge into Hallows End, I immediately hear someone yelling my name.

"Jonas! Help, Jonas!"

I rush to where Robert Akerman stands near my cabin.

"I am here." I drop the books by my doorstep as the man hurries to me. "What troubles you, Robert?"

"I searched for you everywhere," he says, trying to catch his breath. "Jonas, it's Rebecca."

My eyes narrow. This is...*different.* It's never happened before.

"What has happened?"

"She is giving birth this morn."

I simply stare at the other man.

Rebecca has been pregnant for three hundred and thirty years.

And she's never given birth before.

"Let us go," I reply and immediately run behind the other man to their cottage on the other side of the village.

I can hear her screams of despair. Goddess, how I wish I could bring the advancements of medicine to these people.

"Jonas," Rebecca breathes. "Help me."

Rushing to the end of the bed, I do my best to bring

everything I know about childbirth to the forefront of my mind.

"It has been so long," I mutter and dig my fingers into the skin of my forehead.

"Elisabeth York had her baby just three months past," Robert reminds me, and all I can do is nod.

That baby was born centuries ago for me. For them, it's been mere months.

"Okay, Robert, please put a pot of water on the fire to boil. We also need clean cloths."

He nods and, happy to be given a task, hurries off to complete it.

Rebecca writhes in pain on the bed, and I feel sweat dripping down the middle of my back.

Help me. Lucy, wake up and help me, please.

Rebecca cries out and reaches for my hand. Her stomach is rock-hard, and when I reach between her legs, I can feel the baby's head.

Wake up, Lucy.

What's happening? Where are you?

Hallows End. A baby is being born, and I need your help. Please, come.

I'm on my way.

I can feel Lucy running through her house to get dressed, and then she's sprinting out her back door to the bridge.

"Robert, I have a friend visiting from a neighboring village. She is near my cabin. Please, go get her and bring her to help me here."

He nods and runs away.

A man is coming to bring you to me.

I see him, is her reply.

"Rebecca, I need you to focus. Take a long, deep breath."

"I cannot."

"Yes, you can. With me, now." I inhale deeply, keeping her pretty eyes on mine. "Come now. You can do this. I know you can."

She breathes with me as Lucy and Robert burst through the door. Lucy's eyes are full of concern and a little bit of fear as she joins me.

"I take it this is new?"

"Very."

We work together over the next hour to help Rebecca breathe and push, and then once the baby is born and crying, we clean her up and deal with the afterbirth.

Rebecca and Robert are all smiles as they gently wrap their new son in a blanket that Rebecca made for him.

Once I'm sure the baby and mother are safe and healthy, Lucy and I take our leave, walking back to my cabin.

Once inside, Lucy sighs and drops into one of my chairs.

"Holy crap, Jonas."

"My thoughts exactly." I wave my hand, and the hearth fire lights. I need tea.

"So, let me get this straight," she continues as she

wipes her hands over her face, "that poor woman has been pregnant since *forever*?"

"Pretty much."

"That's...that's...I can't even. I literally can't even imagine it. And now, for some reason that we can't figure out, she's had the baby."

"Yes." I pace to the window, my mind full of jumbled thoughts. "I don't know how it's possible. Nothing ever changes here, Lucy. *Nothing.* It's the same conversations, the same movements, the same weather. William Northrup is a boy of seven, and he gets an ear ache every month."

"Does anyone die, over and over again?"

My gaze turns to her, and my shoulders fall.

"Mrs. Horton. She's ninety-two, and each month, she has a heart attack."

"For fuck's sake," Lucy mutters and shakes her head. "We're meeting with the others at Xander's house later today. Maybe they'll have some ideas as to what's going on."

"I'm sorry that I dragged you over here," I say. "I put you at risk. But it has been so long since I've assisted in a birth. I panicked. That's unlike me."

"They'll forget I was here in just a few days," she reminds me while reaching out to take my hand, twining our fingers. I feel the energy pulse between us. "And then she'll be pregnant again. Goddess, she went through all of that for nothing."

She turns tortured eyes to me, and her hand tightens.

"This has to end, Jonas. We're going to figure this out because Rebecca should *not* have to give birth, month after month. And Mrs. Horton needs to rest in peace."

"I can't even express how much I agree with you."

Before I forget, I pull my Book of Shadows out of the lower drawer of my desk and add it to a small pile of texts I want to bring back to Salem with me.

"I have to stay here for the day," I inform her. "I want to be around if Rebecca needs me or in case anything else happens."

"Maybe you should start sleeping here at night again."

"No." I shake my head, leaving no room for argument. "I won't leave you, not at night. You're too vulnerable then."

"But these are your people, Jonas. And they need you."

"Do you think I wouldn't choose you?" My voice is harsh, almost ragged. "That if it came down to it, you wouldn't be the one I'd choose, over and over again? What is the new term? Ah, yes. Fuck that, Lucy. You are my priority, and you will be until the day I finally get to die."

"Don't say it like that." She climbs onto my lap and loops her graceful arms around my neck. "Don't. Because if I lost you now, I don't think I could survive it, Jonas."

I press my forehead to hers, and we sit in the silence, just holding each other as the sun rises.

"Why do I feel like something big is coming?" Her voice is a whisper.

"Because it is." I sigh and gently press my lips to hers. "It is."

She nods and then pulls back, and I can hear her talking to Nera in her mind.

Don't worry, I'm coming soon. All is well.

"He worries."

"If he's not with me, he's a nervous wreck," she admits with a small smile. "He's really a mother hen."

"I'm glad. If I can't be next to you all the time, I'm relieved that he *is*. Don't go anywhere without him from now on, at least until we get this figured out."

She raises an eyebrow, and it makes me smile. "So, you think you can just boss me around now or something? Just because I'm in love with you?"

And, just like that, my heart stops, and the breath leaves my lungs.

Those green eyes of hers grow big as if she's shocked that she said the words out loud.

My fingertips dance down her cheek and then over her neck, finally plunging into her beautiful, thick hair.

"The love I feel for you is at once life-affirming and terrifying, Luciana. It is with every fiber of my being that I love you. I'm entirely under your spell, and my heart is yours to keep."

Tears glitter in her eyes as she swallows hard and then offers me a watery smile.

"Well, that might be the most romantic thing anyone has ever said in the history of the world."

"I mean every word of it. I have waited centuries for you."

"Damn." She swipes at a tear. "Seventeenth-century men know how to treat a woman."

I smile as she cleans up the tears and then takes my hand to press it to her cheek.

"Be careful today," she says. "I'll be in the shop with Nera until closing, and then we will go to Xander's."

"I'll be there in time to join you for that," I assure her. "And *you* be cautious, as well."

"Oh, I am," she promises. "I'll be on my toes. Now, I'm going to sneak out before the village becomes too active."

I pull her in for a quick hug. "Thank you for coming."

"If you call for me, I'll come. That's just how it works."

With one last squeeze, she pulls back and then winks at me.

"I'll see you soon."

I step out to watch her hurry to the tree line. At the bridge, she turns and blows me a kiss, and then she's gone.

I'll see you soon, she says once more in my mind.

Very soon, indeed.

"I brought pizza," Giles announces as he walks into Xander's home library. He sets the stack of boxes on a table and pushes his glasses up his nose, eyes immediately searching for Breena.

Breena frowns at the book she's reading.

"I'm *so* hungry," Lorelei says with a grateful smile and opens the top box. "Who likes anchovies?"

"I do." Xander shoulders her out of the way to take a slice.

"The others don't have fish," Giles assures her. "Okay, so, what are we doing?"

"Just chilling," Lucy replies with a sweet smile. "Getting to know each other better. Discussing what we're going to wear to Friday night's dance."

Giles's eyes narrow. "You're a smartass, Lucy Finch."

"We're researching," Xander says with his mouth full. "I have a few books over there to go through, all from the eighteen hundreds. Basically, we're searching for anything that might mention the curse, the town, or anything we think might correlate with what's going on in Hallows End."

"Essentially," Lorelei adds and licks tomato sauce from the corner of her mouth, "we're searching for a needle in an ocean of hay. That's more than a haystack."

"I'm also hitting up message boards." Breena opens her laptop. "Reaching out to people I know but being careful in how I word things. Don't worry, I won't set off any alarms or anything."

"I trust you," I assure her and eye the pizza.

"Grab some," Lucy suggests. "Bambolina is the *best.*"

"I honestly don't usually eat in Salem," I admit.

"Why? The food's great," Lorelei replies.

"Mostly out of solidarity. I have a sense of loyalty to those in Hallows End who eat the same things, day in and out. It's hardly fair that I can come here and eat this kind of food and they cannot. However, I'm starving, so I'll eat."

I snag a slice and return to my chair.

"Now that everyone's here, we can fill you in on what happened this morning," Lucy announces and shoves the last of her pizza into her mouth.

I can't resist reaching over to brush a crumb from her lips.

"Tell us," Breena says.

I relay everything that transpired from the minute I crossed the bridge into Hallows End until Lucy returned to her home afterward.

"She's been pregnant for *three centuries*?" Lorelei demands and swallows hard.

"That's what I said," Lucy agrees.

"I don't like that things are *different*." I shake my head slowly. "It has been *exactly* the same since the night I cast the curse. There's never been a deviation. Until today."

"Maybe because we're working and digging into it? Perhaps we...unstuck something," Breena suggests. "Like when you're trying to loosen something, and you wiggle it around until it starts to give."

"I think that's exactly what's happening," Xander says, speaking for the first time. "Also, Jonas, did you realize that you have three hundred and thirty-three years, to the minute, to break the curse?"

I scowl at the other man. "That can't be accurate."

"From what I've read, it *is*. The curse remains in place for those three hundred and thirty-three years, and then it's simply *done*."

"What happens to Hallows End and all the people there?" Lucy asks.

"They're gone," I say before Xander can. His sober, dark eyes tell me I'm right. "Wiped off the Earth as if they never were."

"Yes," Xander agrees.

"Absolutely fucking *not*." Lucy stands to pace.

"Hey, don't worry," Lorelei says and takes Lucy's hand in hers. "It's been three hundred and thirty years. Right, Jonas?"

"Almost thirty-one," I reply. "Come Samhain."

"That leaves us with two whole years to get this right," Lorelei insists. "We have plenty of time."

I can't help but laugh. When all eyes turn to me, I take a breath and shrug. "You have no idea how quickly time passes."

"But time doesn't really exist," Giles adds. "It's something we use here in this realm, but it doesn't exist, so it shouldn't factor in."

"I like that philosophy, but the truth is, we do use time in this realm, and it absolutely does factor in here," Xander replies. "And I agree with Jonas, time goes fast. Two years sounds like a long time, but it'll move quicker than we want it to."

"Great," Breena mutters. "So, not only do we have to catch a killer, but we also have a deadline on lifting the curse. No pressure or anything."

"I've said it before, and I'll say it again. If you don't want to—or can't—help me, I understand."

"Oh, no," Breena says and stands to reach out to me, taking my hand. "That's not at all what I meant. We *will* help. It's just frightening. And, honestly, intimidating. But it's going to happen, Jonas. You're our family now."

"You are perhaps the kindest soul I've ever met, Breena."

Her cheeks flush from the compliment, and then she returns to her computer.

"I have a woman I can reach out to in Louisiana." Lucy pulls at her bottom lip. "She's possibly the most powerful being I've met, and she's just wonderful. I'll call her first thing in the morning."

"Miss Sophia?" Xander asks quietly.

"Yes."

"Good thinking. Giles, were you able to get that tiger's eye sphere we spoke about last night at your shop?"

"Yes," Giles replies, fishing around in his satchel for the crystal. "I knew that a friend of mine in Boston would have it. So, after we spoke, I called him and then drove over to pick it up."

"Excellent, thank you."

"After you came to Breena's?" Lucy asks, and Giles frowns at her.

"I wasn't at Breena's last night."

Now, both Breena and Lucy scowl at the man.

"You knocked right on my door, Giles," Breena says, addressing him for the first time. "Right after you tried to call me."

"I *did* try to call," he admits. "Because you won't freaking talk to me, and it's damn frustrating. But I can assure you, I was *nowhere* near your house. I had to go into Boston, and traffic into the city is always a bitch."

Lucy and Breena share a look that's full of confusion.

"What happened?" Xander demands.

"We were in my house," Breena begins, "talking and such, and my phone rang. I dismissed Giles's call, but then there was a knock on the door. It was Giles. It didn't really surprise me because I've been dodging him for a few days."

"We *are* going to talk," Giles assures her, but she ignores him, and Lucy picks up the story.

"Breena wouldn't invite him in. Oh, my goddess, Breen. You *refused* to welcome him in, and he even mentioned it."

"What did he say?" Xander asks.

"'*You won't invite me in?*' That's what he said. And

Breena said no and told him to go. Thank the goddess you didn't invite him—or *it*—in."

"What was it, if it wasn't Giles?" Breena demands. "I know what Giles looks like. I've had a crush on him for my entire adult life, remember?"

"For fuck's sake," Giles murmurs under his breath.

"This isn't the first time one of you has had contact with this," I say. "Lucy, you saw the dog in the night when you were walking with Nera."

"That was no dog," she counters. "It had human eyes."

"It can't be a skinwalker." Xander scrubs his hand through his dark hair. "It just can't be."

"What in the ever-loving hell is a *skinwalker*?" Giles demands.

"I don't think we want to know," Lorelei says. "It sounds creepy as hell."

"Oh, it's worse than that," I reply.

CHAPTER TWELVE
LUCY

"It literally *cannot* be," Xander insists, and Jonas shakes his head.

"Why?" I ask. "Why can't it be?"

"Because based on everything I've ever read or have been told, skinwalkers are a Navajo legend. They're witches who can take the form of an animal, not a *person*, and they're creepy as fuck. They don't just take the shape of the dog or animal. They're not a typical shifter. They're malevolent, and they look as such."

"That red dog I saw looked pretty damn malevolent," I mutter and reach down to pet Nera, who hasn't left my side all day. "And I think it's safe to say that I can now consider myself an expert on such things."

"Yeah, no one suggested this was a good thing," Lorelei adds.

"That's not what I meant. I'm just saying, there

aren't many Navajo in this area. At least, that I'm aware of."

"Doesn't mean they aren't here," Giles says. "Although why anyone would be here for a couple of hundred years just to kill one witch each year is beyond me."

"Maybe they don't *live* here," I suggest. "Maybe they just come here from wherever and then leave once the job is done."

"Like a hitman?" Breena asks with a frown. "That seems weird, even for us."

"Generations of Navajo witches, making the journey to Salem just to kill one of us every year. That doesn't seem plausible." Giles looks over to Breena. "You're right."

"But it *could* be any witch who can shift," Lorelei points out, frowning at Xander. "Just because you choose things like cats and birds doesn't mean that someone with a dark spirit couldn't or wouldn't do creepier things. Are *you* considered a skinwalker? Isn't it just another term for shifter?"

"I'm absolutely not a skinwalker," Xander says, shaking his head emphatically. "What I do isn't meant to hurt anyone or impact them in any way. It's just a form of transmogrification. But what you suggest could happen. I think we're quickly learning that *anything* can happen."

"You know what?" I decide right on the spot. "Screw waiting for tomorrow morning to call Miss Sophia. I'm calling now."

I reach for my phone, open my contacts, page down to her name, and hit FaceTime.

After just a few moments of ringing on the other end, Sophia answers, and her sweet smile is a balm to my overstimulated nervous system.

"Well, Lucy. How lovely to see you." But her eyes narrow on my face. "Oh, dear."

"Yeah. It's lovely to see you, too, but this isn't just a leisurely phone call. We'll do that soon."

"I hope so. How can I help?"

"Well, first of all, I'm not here alone. I have a room full of people with me."

I introduce the others one at a time, stopping when I get to Jonas.

"This is Jonas. And what I'm about to tell you is a story that you may not believe."

"I'd like to hear this story."

The others are quiet as Jonas and I tell Sophia about the curse of the blood moon. When we're finished, Sophia blinks, takes a deep breath, and then blows it out slowly.

"This is absolutely fascinating," she says at last. "I can't say it's anything I've heard of before, but I'm in a very different part of the country. Let me ask around and do some reading."

She scowls as if she's frustrated.

"What is it?" Xander asks her.

"Well, it's peculiar. I'm completely blocked when I try to reach out and speak with Jonas's guides or ancestors. It's like the phone is just...disconnected. That's not unheard of, but it is rare for me. I want you all to be *very* careful. This isn't the kind of curse you simply play with. It's powerful. More than any of us realize. I can feel that much. But it's also not the only reason you're reaching out to me tonight."

"No," I agree. "We're also calling because of some other weird things that have been happening in Salem."

"It's almost Samhain, child," she reminds me. "Of course, things are happening. And I hope you've reinforced your protective shields."

"We have," I rush to assure her. "And will continue to do so. But I have questions about skinwalkers."

Miss Sophia's eyes sharpen and narrow, and before she can ask questions, I tell her about the red dog and the fake Giles showing up at Breena's home.

"Excuse me," Miss Sophia says and sets down the phone. I glance at the others in surprise as we hear running water and see lights start to flicker around the room.

She lit candles.

"I'm sorry," she says when she returns. "I needed to reinforce my protections here. What you speak of is not something I've ever heard your mother or aunts talk about before."

"Us, either," I agree.

"But we've never been a target before," Breena adds. "Miss Sophia, could things like this have happened to

Agatha and the hundreds of others who were murdered before, but they just didn't say anything to anyone?"

"Agatha would have told her sisters," Miss Sophia insists, completely dismissing anything to the contrary. "I can't imagine that any witch *wouldn't* confide in someone they trust after seeing something like that. It has to be frightening."

"What if they didn't know?" Xander asks. "What if they didn't realize that's what they were seeing?"

"Possible," she says slowly. "But unlikely."

"We didn't know that the *thing* at Breena's door wasn't Giles," I insist. "Miss Sophia, it was Giles in every way—his mannerisms, even his voice."

"But Giles would never have said, '*you won't invite me in*?' He never would have asked it that way."

"No," Giles agrees. "I wouldn't have."

"But it's not until *now* that you realized that," I add. "Breena, in that moment, you would have sworn that Giles was at your door. All I'm saying is it could be that any of the previous targets, my mother included, didn't realize that the *thing* speaking to them wasn't the person they knew and trusted."

"You make a good point," Miss Sophia says. "And you may be right. But just like I'm being blocked regarding the curse, I can't see what's happening with this murderer either. I'll try harder and keep you posted. In the meantime, Lucy, I have something for you. Years ago, I visited Salem when you were quite young, and your mother asked me to hold onto something for you until the time came that you needed it."

I blink at her, feeling tears prick the backs of my eyes. "What is it?"

"She warned me that you're not the most patient woman. Don't worry, I'll send it to you, but I don't trust any shipping company. My granddaughter, Lena, and her husband are leaving tomorrow to embark on a journey. Mason is an archeologist, and there's a new dig in Burma with a huge discovery of Painite, an elusive crystal. Mason is beside himself."

"I think I'm beside *myself*," Giles says, his eyes alight at the news of a rare crystal. "I hope I'll get to ask him some questions."

Breena rolls her eyes, but Miss Sophia continues.

"I'll have Lena and Mason stop there on their way out of the country. I just don't trust this package with anyone else."

"Thank you." I smile at the kind older woman. "For everything."

"I wish I had been more help. I'll do some thinking on my end. Good luck to all of you. Keep your wits about you. I'll talk to you soon."

She ends the call, and I glance around at everyone in the room.

"I hate surprises," I announce and set my phone on the table. "Like, *hate*."

"Is that so?" Jonas asks with a raised eyebrow, and I can't help but laugh and reach out for his hand.

"Except for you. *You* were a great surprise. I just want to know what my mother could have possibly given Miss Sophia for me when I was a kid."

I eye Lorelei.

"Can't you just ask her?"

"Nope," Lorelei says with a shrug. "She just told me not to ask her anything."

"I *hate* that I can't see her." My frustration is growing. "I need her. I have so many questions, and it pisses me off that so many of you can talk to her, but I can't. Even Jonas can see her."

"Not now," he clarifies. "I could at your aunts' house, but not outside of it."

"Still, you *could*. Why is she hiding herself from me? It feels like such a betrayal." I sniffle a little but shake my head when Jonas wraps his arm around my shoulders. "No, it's fine. I'm fine. We have bigger worries here. What should we do next?"

"What we've been doing," Xander says. "It's going to be a process of research and from that research, elimination of what will work and what won't as far as the curse is concerned."

"And the other?" Lorelei asks. "Because although the curse is absolutely a priority, we're nearing Samhain and the time when another witch will die if we don't act quickly."

"Same goes," Giles answers. "Keep our protections and guards up. Refresh those wards. Don't invite *anything* inside your home. And stay aware."

"Limbo," Breena says with a sigh. "I've always hated being in limbo. But it'll all work out, you guys. We're going to figure it all out."

"I love your optimism," Lorelei says and reaches for Breena's hand. "I love *you*. Don't hate me, okay?"

Breena just laughs and then shrugs her shoulders. "I don't think I'm capable of hating anyone. Or staying mad for too long."

"A beautiful soul," Jonas murmurs, echoing his thoughts from earlier.

"Good, then we can talk," Giles says.

"Later," Breena replies, looking resigned. "After the rest is figured out."

"Bullshit," Giles counters, but his voice is perfectly calm. "That could take a while, and I have things to say. So, if the others will excuse us, I'd like to ask Breena to join me for a walk."

"If I knew how bossy you are, I probably wouldn't have had a crush on you," Breena says as she stands from the table and walks ahead of Giles out of the library.

Giles simply turns back to us and winks.

"That's so sweet," I say with a sigh. "They're going to make beautiful babies together."

"She's barely speaking to him," Xander reminds me. "Let's get to the dating stage before you start counting second cousin nieces and nephews."

"It's gonna happen," Lorelei adds, agreeing with me. "And it kind of makes me emotional. And I'm an ice queen."

"No, you're not," Xander replies quietly.

The room is thick with tension until Jonas clears his throat and stands. "I'll just go grab a book and dig into the research."

"Me, too."

I don't like the dreams.

And I know that I'm dreaming, but I can't seem to pull myself out of it.

"Don't go down that road."

I spin in the middle of the street and find my mother standing behind me, but her face looks...wrong.

"Mom?"

"Don't do it," she says again. "I can't save you if you do."

"I'm not hurt."

"You will be. Stop walking."

I look down and see that my feet are moving without me even realizing it. "I'm not trying to."

"Luciana, do as I say. Stop it, right now."

"I can't." I look up and reach out for her, but she's gone. "Mom? Mom! I can't stop."

"You'll die."

The words are an echo in my mind. I search around me, but there's no one there.

"I will not! Mom? Help!"

Water. Water's flowing around my ankles, and my

feet are sinking into the concrete below as if it's turned into sand and I'm on the shoreline.

Because I am *at the shoreline.*

"How did I get here?"

"Lucy?"

My heart is beating so hard, it feels like it's going to explode.

"Lorelei! I'm over here!"

"Lucy?" She calls and calls as if I'm lost, but I'm standing twenty yards away from her. "Where did you go?"

"I'm right here!*" I try to run to her, but my feet are stuck in the sand, and the water is rising. "Help me get out of this."*

But she doesn't hear me.

"Lucy!"

Breena and Giles come rushing out of the woods.

"We can't find her," Giles says, his face white, and his expression grim. "She's not anywhere in the forest."

"And the bridge is gone," Breena adds as Xander, in the form of a raven, lands on a log and then changes into his human form.

"She can't have just disappeared." His voice is edged with both anger and fear. "Where's Jonas?"

"Gone," Lorelei whispers. "Just gone. And I can't find Lucy."

"I'm here!" For the love of Thor, why can't they hear me? "Just help me! I'm stuck!"

"They got her." Breena buries her face in Giles's chest to

weep. "Oh, goddess, what will we do without our Lucy? She won't meet our baby."

Her hands smooth over her rounded belly.

Breena's pregnant?

"I'm here." I'm crying now, trying to reach them with my mind since they can't hear my voice. "Please, I'm right here. I love you. Help me."

Suddenly, I'm plunged into blackness. Into nothing.

There's no beginning and no end. No light. And I feel so cold and alone.

"Where am I?"

The words echo back to me.

"Hello?"

I blink.

And look into terror.

"Lucy."

I'm screaming and flailing, trying to run, but strong arms hold me tight, and Jonas's voice is in my ear now.

"Only a dream, baby. It's just a horrible dream."

"Don't touch me." I squirm away and then fall to the floor, backing myself into the corner of the room, my knees pulled up to my chest. I need to make myself small. To hide.

"Luciana."

His voice isn't gentle now, it's strong, and I look into his blue eyes.

"It wasn't real," he says, still in that firm tone. "It's not now."

My chest is heaving as I try to catch my breath. I have

goose bumps all over my body, and Nera, my sweet Nera, carefully joins me and nudges me with his head.

Love you, he says in my mind.

I bury my face in his fur and give in to the sobs of grief and worry leftover from the dream.

Finally, Jonas simply joins me on the floor and holds us both. He's whispering, and from what I can hear, it sounds like a spell of calming and protection.

After what feels like forever, I start to warm up, and the tears stop.

"I hate the dreams," I say at last.

"Darling, that wasn't a dream." His voice is grim. "That was a premonition. One I don't plan on letting come true."

"Oh, goddess." I tip my head onto his shoulder. "I'm so tired, but I'm afraid to sleep."

"You're safe." He kisses the top of my head. "Will you let me put you back to bed so you can rest?"

"Nera, too."

He nods, and the three of us climb onto the bed, huddled together.

And with the protection of my boys, I slide into a dreamless sleep.

"Y**ou're here."** I bounce on my toes and then rush across my shop to scoop Lena up into a big hug. "Oh, it's so good to see you."

"Same here." She squeezes me. "When Gram asked us to stop by, I was *so* excited. Salem's awesome, and so are you."

"Where's Mason?" I glance behind her, but I don't see him in the doorway. "Did you ditch him somewhere?"

"He's just getting the box out of the car," she explains. "I hear you guys have a lot going on."

"More action than any of us wants," I agree and smile at Mason when he walks in holding a box about the size of a shoebox. "Hey, Mason."

"Hi, Lucy." He smiles and leans in to kiss my cheek as he passes me the box. "There, it's out of my hands and no longer my responsibility."

"Gram kind of put the fear of the goddess into us about what would happen should anything happen to that." She points at the box. "We're happy to pass it on."

"How long are you in town?"

"Just the day. We have a flight first thing tomorrow."

"Well, I have a friend named Giles who is *dying* to talk with Mason. He's a rock nerd."

"*Nice.* Just tell me where to find him, and I'll head that way while you two chat."

"His shop is called Gems. It's on Essex Street."

"Great. I'll see you later." He pulls his wife in for a kiss, nods to me, and then he's gone again.

"Marriage looks good on you."

Lena grins. "Thanks. Listen, I know you're dying to open that box, so if you'll point me to your restroom, I'll leave you be so you can have a moment with your mama."

"Thanks. It's just back there."

When Lena takes off in search of the bathroom, I open the box and smile at the envelope on top.

In my mom's handwriting, it says: *Luciana.*

I blow out a breath and open the letter, but a bunch of customers come into the shop, and I'm distracted for a while until Delia comes in to help.

"Okay, I'm going to help Delia," Lena announces, surprising me. "Go look at your stuff. I mean it."

She practically shoos me out of my own place, but I don't put up much of a fight.

And when I'm alone in my kitchen, with Nera lying on his bed near the back door, I open the letter.

My sweet girl,

I knew that if I held onto this, I'd be tempted to give it to you much sooner than was right, so I asked an old friend to hang on to it for me. To take the temptation away. Because, like you, I'm an impatient woman.

I know that by the time you read this, I'll be gone. Well, my body will, anyway. I'm sure I'm still living contentedly with my sisters and looking after you and your cousins, but I'm no longer of this Earth.

I know you're angry, but it's the way it was meant to be, and there was no stopping it.

I'm going to say that again because I know you'll be blaming yourself, thinking that there was something you could have done. But believe me when I say, there was absolutely nothing *to be done.*

You're also angry because you can't see me.

I gasp and cover my mouth with my hand.

I know you. But, my darling girl, if I came to you all the time, it would become meaningless. You'll see me when you need it the most. You need to remember that even though you can't see or hear me, I'm always with you. Always. And when it comes time for you to be strong, you will prevail.

You will have help. You will win.

I love you so deeply that I ache with it, my sweet. You are the light of my life, and the best thing that I ever did. If you need me, all you have to do is call for me.

Always yours,

Mom

I read it twice and then simply sit at the table and rest my head on my arms as I cry.

"You've cried too often since I've known you."

Jonas's hands are on my shoulders. I simply pass him the letter and let the tears come.

CHAPTER THIRTEEN

He stands on the street, in front of the house where she lives, watching. The wards are strong enough to keep him back, and that sparks an anger in him that he hasn't felt in centuries.

How *dare* she?

Now, he has to find another way to get to her. The inconvenience will only add to the satisfaction when he takes her life, though.

He watches as those inside laugh, and a smile slowly spreads across his face.

He will wipe the laughter off all their faces.

He glances to his left.

"You'll do."

Chapter Fourteen
Jonas

"There is no mention of the three-hundred-and-thirty-three-year deadline that Xander mentioned the other night," I inform Lucy as she comes behind her counter to hold items for her last customer of the day. "I've read through my Book of Shadows and the one my aunt gave me before she passed, and it's not there."

Lucy chews on her lip in thought. "Maybe what Xander read is wrong. I mean, the information is hundreds of years old and could have been mistranslated or something."

"It came from somewhere." I can hear the frustration in my voice as Lucy turns away to help her customer. I don't know why I'm fixated on this point, other than I don't know how I missed it so long ago.

Again, I've asked myself, would it have changed anything in the moment? Probably not.

But I *know* I wouldn't have missed it before.

"Hey, I have a delivery for you."

I glance up at the voice at the door. Lucy smiles at the delivery person.

"Oh, hi. Great, I was waiting for those. You can just leave it there. I'll get it."

"I don't mind bringing it in for you," he says. "But it's not heavy."

"Yeah, it's no worries. Thank you."

"Have a good one." He scans the box with his tool and then waves and hurries off.

Lucy finishes ringing up the customer's order and then walks her to the door so she can pull the box in and lock up for the day.

"I had a fun day today," Lucy says with a smile as she carries the box to the counter and sets it down. "The customers were all interesting and needed such diverse things for their practices. I so enjoy helping them make their choices."

"You're good with them," I confirm and close the book before me so I can give Lucy all my attention. "And they respect you, as they should. You know what you're doing."

"I studied for a long time." She flashes a small smile. "This shop didn't happen on a whim or because I thought it would be a fun hobby. I studied herbs and plants for *years*. I spent so much time in the kitchen trying to come up with the salves and tinctures, the drinking teas and the bath teas."

"I'd never heard of a bath tea," I admit.

"Water is powerful, as we know. And when you add the right herbs and salt with the perfect intention to the bath, it can create an intense spell. *Everyone* knows the benefits of Epsom salts, right?"

"Do they?" I ask and cross my arms, enjoying her.

"Well, in the modern world, they do. Now, add in rose and lavender and other things, depending on the intention, and it's just"—she kisses her fingers—"chef's kiss. And it smells good, too."

"You always smell good."

I reach for her and pull her against me, burying my nose in her red hair and breathing deeply.

"See? Bath teas work."

Suddenly, she looks up at me. "I have an idea."

"Yes, I'd love to join you for a bath."

Lucy laughs. "Later. First, I just realized I don't have a photo of you. None. Let's take a selfie."

"What in the world is a *selfie*?"

She narrows her eyes on me. "You're kidding, right? I mean, I know that most of the time you live in 1692, but you move between both places. A selfie is a photo that you take of *yourself*."

"Ah." I kiss the tip of her nose. "Makes perfect sense when you put it like that."

"Have you *ever* had your photo taken?"

"Not to the best of my knowledge. I did once sit for a portrait when I was a boy."

She blinks at me slowly. "Wow. You're old."

Now, my lips twitch. She's in a wonderful mood this afternoon.

"How do we go about this *selfie* business?" I ask her as she settles herself in my lap and pulls her cell out of the pocket of her dress.

"It's super painless," she replies, waking up the phone. "Just smile at that little dot right there."

"Must I smile?"

Her face whips to mine. "Why wouldn't you?"

"What if I want to...*smolder*."

Lucy laughs and then kisses my cheek. "Do whatever makes you happy. Ready?"

She holds up the phone, and I look at the dot.

She takes the picture.

"Another," she says, and before she presses the button to capture the image, she turns and kisses my cheek.

"Aww, look how adorable we are." She shows me the photo, and I smile.

"Precious," I reply, enjoying the banter. "Do it again."

With a smile, she raises the camera, and I turn her face to mine and kiss her lips.

"*Nice*," she says when she examines the resulting image. Suddenly, she frowns and looks over her shoulder. "Did you hear that?"

I shake my head and follow her gaze. "No, what did it sound like?"

"I don't know, just a noise. Must be the wind.

Anyway, do you know what one of the perks of you not having a phone is?"

"I couldn't possibly guess."

"No dick pics."

I blink at her. "Pardon?"

"Dick pics." She sets her phone on the countertop. "They're *so* annoying. But you don't send them."

"I'm afraid to ask, but what is that, exactly?"

Her eyes dance as she drags her fingertip down the front of my shirt. "It's when a man takes a photo of his fully erect penis and sends it to a woman via text as sort of an...invitation."

"An invitation for what?"

Her lips twitch. "For sex, Jonas."

"I admit, I'm out of the loop a bit when it comes to modern relationships. We didn't *date* back in the day, but I have to ask."

"Ask whatever you like. I'm enjoying this immensely." She settles more squarely in my lap, rests her elbow on my shoulder, and plops her chin in her hand. "I'll tell you everything I know."

"Do women actually *enjoy* receiving those photos?"

"Oh, not at all."

I blink at her. "Then why, pray tell, do men send them?"

She purses her lips in thought. "Well, I'm not a man, so I can only guess, but I *think* the thought process is that the man with the dick in question thinks it's so impressive that if he snaps a photo of it and sends it to the person he would *like* to bed, that the receiver will be so overcome with lust and desire that the sex is a done deal at that point."

"And despite not liking the photos, does it work?"

"I can only speak for me, but no. Absolutely not."

"And how many of these have you received?"

Her lips twitch. "Admittedly, only one. In college."

"What happened to the days of courting a woman? Showing her affection and having a conversation?"

"Well, I think that still happens sometimes. But so do the dick pics."

"Interesting." I kiss her nose. "I don't think I'd be one for doing that."

Her arms wrap around my neck, and she cuddles closer, igniting the fire inside me that never goes out when it comes to Luciana.

"I don't think you would, either. I do, however, have an idea."

"I can't wait to hear it."

She presses her lips to my cheek and then my lips. "Perhaps we should go take one of my good-smelling baths so I can see your...*dick*...in real life rather than in a photo. I suspect that would work *very* well on me."

"Well, then." I lift her out of the chair and immediately set off for the stairs that lead to her private bathroom. "Let's see what we can do."

"**B**reena should be here any minute," Lucy announces as she hurries down the steps and into her shop, fastening a pair of earrings.

All I can do is stare at her.

"What? Did my makeup smear again? I don't usually wear it, but Breena wants to try out her new camera, and—"

She breaks off as I step to her, frame her face in my hands, and simply devour her mouth.

"I don't have time for this," she says against my lips. "No matter how sexy you are, I don't have time."

"You're the most beautiful woman in the world."

"Maybe I should wear makeup more often."

I smile. "It's the whole ensemble put together. The gown, the hair, the makeup. You're a goddess."

"Aww, how sweet." This is followed by the sound of the shutter on a camera.

Our heads turn at Breena's voice.

"That's gonna be a framer," Breena decides, looking down at the back of her camera. "Wow, Jonas, you *do* show up on film."

Lucy laughs as she pulls away from me. "He's not a vampire, Breen."

"Hey, you never know. But now, we do. Okay, so let's start with photos inside the shop, and then we'll go outside."

"Perhaps I'll go to my cabin while you two have fun with this."

"No, you should stay," Lucy says. "We'll have a few more photos taken of the two of us."

Her eyes are full of humor, but I know there's more to the request than meets the eye.

And I find that I simply can't tell her no.

"Let's start by the wall of herbs," Breena suggests. "Your burnt-orange dress is *perfect* against the green of this wall."

At first, Lucy seems to be self-conscious as she poses, but then she gets into the spirit of things, and the two of them have fun.

"Now I want you to look like you're going to put that lotion on your face," Breena says to Lucy.

"Actually..." Lucy eyes me. "Come here, Jonas. This will be fun."

When I approach, she takes my chin in her fingers and gently brushes the lotion on *my* face, all the while Breena snaps photos.

"That's sexy," Breena says with a sigh. "And will be *so* perfect for your social media. Okay, I think we have enough of the inside. Let's go outside."

Breena gets photos of the sign out front with the Blood Moon Apothecary logo, then the building itself with its deep front porch. And then she asks Lucy to hold her broom and stands on the first step by the sign. Nera sits perfectly at his owner's side.

"Brilliant," Breena murmurs. "Oh, put your fingers in the ends of your hair and look out toward the water as if you're lost in thought or conjuring a witchy spell."

"Are there spells that aren't witchy?" Lucy asks with a half smile but does as she's told. Finally, she crooks her finger at me. "Join me."

I don't know how to pose for a camera, and I feel awkward and foolish.

But rather than face Breena, Lucy simply hugs me, her arms firmly around my shoulders.

This part is easy.

I fold her against me and close my eyes, breathing her in.

I love you, she says in my head. *And I know that I'll have you always, but just in case, I need these images.*

I love you, too. I pull back and press my lips to her forehead. *I'm not going anywhere. We're going to figure all of this out.*

She smiles, nods, and then pulls back to turn to Breena, who wipes a tear from the corner of her eye.

"What's wrong, Breen?" Lucy asks.

"I don't know what the two of you said in your heads, but that was so darn sweet. I think Lorelei will be here soon. We're bringing dinner by so we can all be together."

"I love that," Lucy says with a smile. "One day, we'll all get dressed up like this and have our photo taken together."

"You know I love a witchy vibe." Breena waggles her eyebrows as Lorelei parks in the driveway.

I notice that Breena is wearing a pink dress, and Lorelei has on a purple one.

"I could snap a photo of the three of you now," I offer. "All three of you are lovely. And...what was that term? Ah, yes, *witchy.*"

"Photoshoot!" Lorelei exclaims as she hurries over and wraps her arms around Lucy.

Breena patiently takes a few moments to coach me on how to use her camera, and then the three of them form a line, holding each other's hands.

They look at me, all somber, and I press the button on the camera.

The shutter clicks.

Next, Breena lays her head on Lorelei's shoulder, and Lucy reaches across Lorelei to take Breena's hand.

It's a beautiful action of solidarity that moves me.

These three women are linked by more than blood.

They have spent many lifetimes together.

"I'm hungry," Lucy declares after a few more images. "Let's set up a picnic in the garden. The sunflowers are still blooming."

"That sounds lovely," Breena says, and the four of us gather the supplies that Lorelei brought with her.

When everything is set up outside, I decide to take my leave.

I want the three of them to enjoy some time together alone.

And I have some questions for their mothers.

"I'll be back in a few hours." I tip my head down to kiss Lucy.

"You're not hungry?" she asks with a frown.

"I'll snag something. Don't worry about me. Just reach out if you need me."

I wave, then leave out of the back garden gate to walk the mile or so to the aunts' house.

Astrid already has the door open, waiting for me.

"I didn't call ahead," I say with a smile. "My apologies."

"You never have to call when you're set to visit a couple of psychic witches, honey. We already knew." She gestures for me to come inside. "Hilda and I were just having dinner, and we have plenty to share. I hope you like corn chowder."

"Now that, I know." The house smells like the soup and sends me back several hundred years to when I was a boy in my mother's kitchen.

The grief and homesickness almost knocks me off my feet.

"What's the matter?" Hilda asks with a frown when she sees me. "You don't like corn chowder?"

"I love it," I admit as I sit in a chair at the table. "It just took me back to my mother's kitchen, and I was surprised. I'm not often homesick anymore."

"I'm sorry," Astrid says and reaches up to gently pat my cheek as if I'm her child. "From everything I've read and heard in my research, your mother was a wonderful woman."

"She was," I agree, smiling gratefully. "Thank you."

"So, is this a social call?" Hilda asks. "Not that we

mind when a handsome man wants to have dinner with us. Not at all."

"I do enjoy your company," I reply and smile gratefully when Hilda places a steaming bowl of soup before me. "But I also have questions."

"And here I was hoping to gossip," Astrid says with a sigh. "I heard that Gertrude Griswald from 1834 liked to sacrifice goats in the spring during Litha, and I'm dying to know if that's true."

I laugh and then think back. "Did she have black-and-gray-striped hair?"

"Yes." Astrid leans forward, her eyes shining with anticipation. "And she was married at least seven times."

"Ah, yes, who could forget her? I believe she did kill the goats, but it was only for food. I don't remember anyone saying that it was a ritual situation." I take a bite of the soup.

"Well, that's just boring," Astrid says. "Okay, go ahead and ask your questions. We'll do our best to answer them."

"But we'd still like to sprinkle in more gossip," Hilda reminds us. "So, perhaps we can work out a little trade. Information for information?"

"If I know the answers, I'll share them," I assure her.

"Same goes," Astrid says with a wink. "Now, what's troubling you?"

"I don't know that I'm necessarily troubled," I reply. "I think, more than anything, I'm curious. I've noticed that the three cousins, Lucy, Breena, and Lorelei, share a connection that goes far deeper than being related through family."

"I think that just about anyone, whether they have magic or not, could see that." Hilda nods. "They're incredibly bonded."

"Through how many lifetimes?" I ask, not surprising them in the least. "How many centuries?"

"I don't think it's possible to measure such things that way," Astrid says. "We've always been told by our guides and angels that souls travel in packs, so to speak. We spend our time with the same souls over and over again."

"I believe that all of us have been together for a very long time," Hilda agrees. "But if you're asking if the girls were together in previous lives, we'd say without question they have. Likely many lifetimes."

"Perhaps even one that happened in the late sixteen hundreds?"

They both narrow their eyes in thought.

"It could be." Hilda then turns to her sister. "I wouldn't rule it out."

"What has you curious about this, Jonas?" Astrid asks.

"I may be thinking about everything too much," I admit as I push my empty bowl aside. "But I can't help but wonder if I couldn't lift the curse in the past because Lucy and the others are the key to it. Perhaps they were a part of it before, and I didn't know it."

"And now that you've found them again, you may

have all of the pieces you need to finally prevail?" Astrid finishes for me.

"Yes. That's what I'm thinking."

The two women share a smile.

"That's it, isn't it?"

"We can't reveal too much," Hilda says slowly. "The path of this will happen the way it's meant to, but I will say that you're not on the wrong road of thinking."

"I knew it," I mutter excitedly.

"Now you can answer a question for us," Astrid pipes up. "Do you know what happened to Louisa Mayfield?"

I blink at her and then frown. "Surely, you don't mean Louisa Mayfield from Boston."

"That's the one," Hilda says. "She went missing, and it's been a long-standing cold case in the area. She was in her mid-thirties and unmarried, which was unheard of at that time, and she just suddenly disappeared."

I stand and pace the small kitchen, then go stand by the window and watch as the sun begins to set to the west. "It can't be."

"What is it?"

I turn and stare at them, stupefied.

"Louisa is in Hallows End."

CHAPTER FIFTEEN
LUCY

"We've had such a lovely autumn," Breena says as she lifts her pretty face to the last of the sunshine falling in deep golden rays over her skin. "I know we've had a few days of rain, but for the most part, it's been warm. I don't think I've ever seen the flowers still blooming this close to Samhain."

"Winter will be here soon enough." Lorelei takes a bite of her bruschetta. "And it's usually long and dark. That was one thing that didn't suck about California, the sunshine."

"But you're happy to be home, aren't you?" I ask her.

"Oh, yeah. Home is where the heart is." She stretches her legs out in front of her. We're sitting on a huge quilt that the three of us made together as teenagers. I've hung on to it and use it often for picnics like this one. "But if Xander suddenly moved away, I wouldn't be sad."

"You're doing really well together, all things considered," Breena says. "You hardly ever snipe at each other, and you haven't punched him even once. I consider that progress."

"No physical altercations *is* good," I agree and laugh when Lorelei narrows her eyes speculatively. "Oh, no, now she's thinking about slugging him."

"I already did that once," she says and then jerks a shoulder. "Anyway, enough about *him*. I have to tell you guys that I'm having *such* a good time rediscovering everything that I used to love about the Craft."

"Oh, that makes me so happy." Breena rests her chin in her hand. "Tell us everything. What have you been up to?"

With a smug smile, Lorelei looks around my yard to the fountain I have running in the middle of my vegetable garden, which is about done for the season now, and wiggles her fingers.

To our delight, the water runs much faster and then bubbles up and over the side to slosh onto the ground before I hear her whisper, "*down*," and it all calms to the way it was before.

"You're *so* good at that," I say, shaking my head. "You always were."

"I'm relearning," she admits, returning to her food. "And I'm discovering things about my magic that I didn't know was there before."

"Fascinating," Breena says. "Like what?"

"I don't even know if I can describe it to you. It's

just...I never realized *how* powerful I was until I came home and started studying again. And I know well enough to understand that I can't ever go back. I'll use my powers for the rest of my life. No more turning my back on them, even if Xander makes me want to scream."

"He isn't the center of your powers," I remind her gently. "That's always and forever only *you.*"

She nods and looks back at the fountain. When the water splashes once more, the three of us laugh.

Nera runs over to inspect the water and then takes a drink, which has us laughing even more.

"Poor Nera," Lorelei says. "Come here, good boy."

My familiar hurries over to her and then falls onto his back, right in the middle of the quilt so he can soak up attention from all three of us.

"You know, you never told us what you and Giles talked about the other day when you went on your walk," I remind Breena and watch as her cheeks flush a bright pink. "Oh, it must have been *really good.*"

"Speak," Lorelei demands, still rubbing Nera's belly. "Tell us everything."

"We didn't really say much."

"Right. The blush on your face says *that was a boring conversation.*"

"He wanted to know about the whole crush thing, and he apologized because he didn't know earlier and was worried."

"About what?" Lorelei asks.

"That he may have been careless with his words at

some point and hurt my feelings, but I assured him that he hadn't done anything. He said he'd like to take me out to dinner sometime, and I said he didn't have to."

"Why would you say that?" I ask with a scowl. "Breen, he was asking you on a *date.*"

"Because I don't want him asking me out just because he feels awkward," she says, pushing her fingers through her blond mane of hair. "He feels bad, and I won't be a pity date. That's the *worst.*"

"Okay, for the record, I've seen how he's looked at you since that morning outside your house," I argue. "And he's *not* looking at you with pity on his face."

"I'm such a jerk." Lorelei hangs her head in her hands. "I can't *believe* I said what I did that morning. I made such a mess, and I'm so sorry, Breena."

"Meh, he was going to find out someday." Breena lifts a shoulder, trying to make us believe that she's okay, but embarrassment still hangs all around her. "It's weird how he's decided to always hang around when we're trying to figure out the curse and stuff, though. He never used to do that."

"He's worried about you." I can't help but laugh when Breena just stares at me in confusion.

"Why?"

"Oh, Breena." I reach over and take her hand. "Because whether he sees you as a love interest or his friend, he cares about you, and he knows that we've had some weird shit happening lately."

"He doesn't need to worry," she says. "Can't we work

a spell that makes him forget that he heard what Lorelei said? I'm pretty sure I've seen one written somewhere."

"We can't mess with someone's memories," I remind her. "And you know it."

"Suddenly, she's a stickler for the rules," Breena mumbles, a pout on her pretty pink mouth. "Fine. It doesn't matter. Eventually, he'll lose interest, and things will calm back down again."

"If you say so," Lorelei replies. "Except what if he doesn't lose interest? What if he's...smitten?"

Breena simply snorts and shakes her head. When she looks down, I can see that she's about to change the subject.

"Do you remember, not long after the three of us made this quilt," Breena says, "when we took it out behind Agatha's old house and stood on it and cast that spell?"

The three of us share a look and stand, rooted to the earth through the quilt and our bare feet. We join hands, and in unison, we start to chant.

We are the daughters of daughters.
Our power is multiplied times three.
Wind, earth, and water,
We respectfully call on thee.

The wind swirls around us. The water from the fountain churns, and I can feel the grass and plants growing, reaching for the sky.

What we do is done with love.
What we ask is done with respect.

Hear our call, feel our hearts.

As we will it, so mote it be.

It was an easy little spell we used to do to stir the elements around us, and we all smile at each other, happy that we haven't lost our touch.

"It always felt so invigorating." I take a deep breath. "So *powerful.* Even though it was just a little spell."

"We *are* powerful," Breena reminds me and squeezes my hand before letting go. "And it's good that we're all back together."

"Hey, Lucy, I meant to ask you," Lorelei says as we start to clean up from our dinner. "What did Miss Sophia send from your mom?"

"Oh, my goddess, how did I forget?" Breena says with wide, green eyes. "Yes, tell us what it was."

"Come on. We'll all find out together."

"You didn't open it?" Lorelei asks with surprise.

"I couldn't," I admit. "I read the letter and had a little meltdown. Jonas consoled me, but I decided that I couldn't open the rest without you two with me."

"Well, we're here now." Breena lifts the basket, Lorelei and I fold the quilt, and then the four of us walk into the house through the back door. "Let's go see what Aunt Agatha held onto for you."

"I left it in the shop area so I could keep an eye on it today," I say as we set our things down in the kitchen and move through to the apothecary. "I'm sorry, what did you say?"

Breena frowns at my question.

"I didn't say anything."

I shake my head. Why do I keep thinking that I hear someone speaking? I can't make out the words, but it sounds like I'm missing part of a conversation directed at me.

"Sorry." I flip on the lights when we enter the shop. "I thought you said something. You're welcome to read the letter first, just so we're all on the same page."

Lorelei and Breena huddle together to read the letter, and both have to swipe at tears on their cheeks when they finish.

"Damn," Lorelei mutters. "I sure miss her."

"Me, too," Breena agrees. "That was sweet, and I could hear her voice as I read it. Okay, let's not keep us guessing any longer. Open it up."

I reach into the box and pull out something hard, wrapped in a red velvet cloth. Embroidered on it in black is a protection rune.

"I can feel the power from over here," Lorelei murmurs. "Your mother was a talented witch."

"But not too talented to fall at the hands of a murderer," I reply softly and feel the pain of it as swift and sharp as I did on the morning I found her.

"If you don't unfasten the knot on that package, I'm going to scream," Breena says. "I'm dying of curiosity over here."

With a deep breath, I unfasten the knot in the velvet and fold it over, exposing a dark wooden box.

"I remember this." I run my fingers over the

engraving of my mother's initials on the lid. "My father gave it to her when he asked her to marry him. She said that he was so nervous about it, but he built this for her and engraved it himself."

"That's so sweet," Breena says softly.

"I wondered what'd happened to it after she died because I couldn't find it with her things. Now, I know."

I take a deep breath and lift the lid.

"I don't get it." I take a step back in frustration. "A deck of tarot cards and a pendulum? That's it? No letter with advice or her Book of Shadows, which I also haven't been able to find? Or something else *helpful*?"

"I suspect this *is* helpful, we just don't know how yet," Lorelei says and bites her lip. "Maybe we're supposed to do a tarot reading with the cards. Or use the pendulum."

"I'll have to ask the aunts," I mutter, more than a little disappointed. "I'm getting so tired of *what-ifs*."

"May I hold the cards?" Breena asks, holding her hand out for them. When I pass them to her, her eyes widen. "Wow, I can feel the magic pulsing on them."

"What?" I frown down at them. "I didn't feel anything."

"Here," she says and passes them back to me. "It's like a heartbeat."

But when I hold them in my hands, I don't feel anything at all. It's just...blank.

"I don't feel it. Here, Lorelei, you're the tie breaker."

I pass the deck to her. Immediately, her eyes also

widen. "Wow. Holy shit, Aunt Aggie, you're a damn powerful witch."

"Okay, that's just not fair. And I know she's here because you're talking to her." I scowl at the room at large. "If you're going to block me and not be helpful, you can just *go*, Mom. I love you, but I'm *so mad* at you."

A door slams upstairs, and Lorelei winces.

"She's gone," my cousin informs me. "You two always did fight like cats and dogs."

"It was simply a passionate relationship," Breena says, ever the peacekeeper. "Don't worry, Lucy, you'll feel it when you're supposed to."

I sigh, and before I can reply, Lorelei nods to the box in the corner. "What's in that?"

"Oh, I forgot. It arrived just as I was closing. Breena came to take photos, and I just pushed it to the side. I'm so excited because it took me forever to find just the right piece. You know how I've wanted a nice big piece of moss agate for the shop. A really pretty display piece, you know?"

"You didn't buy it through Giles?" Breena asks and then clears her throat. "Not that such things matter, of course."

I grin at her. "Actually, he found it for me and had it shipped directly here."

I find my box cutter, slice through the tape, and pull out a huge ball of bubble wrap.

"I love that they package these things well, but man,

is it a buzz kill to have to fight your way to the treasure inside," Lorelei mutters.

But between the three of us, we have it unpacked in five minutes.

"Wow," I breathe as I hold the stone in my hands. It's egg-shaped and the size of a football. "It has to weigh fifteen pounds."

"May I?" Breena asks, and when I pass it to her, she frowns. "Huh."

"What is it?" Lorelei asks, but I twirl away, feeling freaking fantastic. "Oh."

"I don't like the way it makes me feel," Breena says.

"Really? Because I think it's *amazing*." I take the piece from Lorelei and press my cheek to the cool, smooth surface. "I can almost *hear* it. As if there's actual moss growing inside. It's so beautiful."

"I don't like this," Lorelei mutters as Breena pulls her phone out of her purse.

"On it," Breena says, but I pay no attention as I dance around the room with the stone. It's as though I'm drunk from it.

I can't get enough.

"I had no idea that having just a huge piece of agate could make my space feel this *euphoric*," I admit with a laugh. "I mean, I know that crystals are powerful, but this is incredible. I guess it's true what they say, bigger *is* better."

"Mom, I need you to send Jonas back right away, please."

"Oh, you don't have to do that." I take the phone from her. "Hi, Aunt Hilda. Everything here is *just fine.* I promise. Jonas can stay there and have fun with you guys. In fact, he can just go on to Hallows End when he's finished. I'm great for tonight. Toodles."

I end the call and pass the phone back to Breena, who just stares at me.

"*Toodles*?" Lorelei demands.

"Oh, loosen up. We should have wine. Do you guys want wine? I don't know why I feel the need to celebrate, but we should. I have some wine in the kitchen."

I hurry through the doorway that leads to my kitchen, the crystal tucked under my arm.

"Don't you just *love* wine?" I frown when I stare around me. I can't seem to remember where I keep it.

"You hate it," Breena insists. "You say it tastes like dead grapes and bad decisions."

I laugh and wag my finger at Breena. "Oh, stop, you big jokester. You're funny, you know that? Where's the wine?"

"You don't keep wine here," Lorelei says. "Why don't you give me the agate to hold onto for you?"

"Absolutely *not.*" I hug it closer to my chest. "Mine. All mine. Do you like moss agate? I thought you were a jasper girl. Or something else oceany."

"I like all the crystals. Do you have your black tourmaline on you, Lucy?"

I narrow my eyes at her. Why does everyone want to

keep me from having fun? Why can't I just be a little carefree sometimes?

"It's around here somewhere. Okay, so I don't have wine, but I do have vodka. That'll do. I even have mint."

Using only one hand, I manage to fill three glasses with ice and pour the vodka over it.

"Hell, who really needs mint?" I ask with a wink and take a long drink from the glass.

"Uh, Lucy, that's straight vodka," Breena says.

"Right? So good. Here, I poured some for you guys. I'm not greedy."

But they don't take the glasses from me, and that makes me mad.

"So, are my refreshments not *good enough* for you two? What the hell?"

"Where is he?" Lorelei asks Breena.

"Where's who?" I demand. "I didn't invite anyone here."

The room is starting to spin, and I drop the stone as I fall into a chair.

I hear it crack.

"Oh, no," I cry. "I broke it."

"Good," I hear Lorelei say, but I can't see her. I can't see either of them now. Why is it so dark? Why is the room spinning?

"Put your head between your knees," Breena says and urges me forward. She rubs circles on my back, and it feels so good.

Suddenly, I just start to cry. I can't help it, and I don't

know why the tears want to come, but I'm a sobbing heap.

Then, I have to run for the bathroom. I'm hugging the toilet, retching, when I hear voices in the hallway.

One of them is deep.

Jonas?

I can't stop throwing up. Sweat runs down my spine and pools at the small of my back. My head is pounding.

I feel sick and lost.

And so alone, even though I can hear them talking.

"Okay." I hear Jonas as he kneels beside me and brushes my hair off my face. "You're going to be okay, darling. Breena's bringing you an ice pack."

"What's happening?"

"We're going to figure that out. Thanks, Breena."

He presses something cold to the back of my neck, and I start to shake, but my stomach begins to settle.

"So tired."

"I know, baby. I know."

CHAPTER SIXTEEN
JONAS

She's still sweaty when I lower her gently to the bed and pull the blankets over her. I wipe at her brow with a rag and wish that I could take away the horrible discomfort.

"Tired," she whispers once more, and I kiss her forehead, then her cheek. I don't like that she feels feverish. "So weird."

"Just sleep," I breathe in her ear. "Nera's here. Nothing's going to hurt you."

She's already drifted off when I look down at the dog, who's been agitated with worry.

"You stay with her while I go back down with Lorelei and Breena. Keep guard, and if anything is wrong, come and get me. Okay?"

The big dog nods and jumps up onto the bed, resting his head on Lucy's chest. He's alert and on guard, and it relieves my mind to know he's here with her. Lucy's hand automatically comes up to stroke Nera's head as though, even in sleep, he brings her comfort.

Secure in the knowledge that he won't leave her side, I return downstairs, where Breena and Lorelei glare at a stone sitting on the kitchen table.

"What, exactly, happened here?"

"That happened," Breena says, pointing to the stone. "Lucy said it was delivered just before she closed. She was expecting it and excited to have it, but when we all opened it, and Lucy touched it, she just...*changed*."

"Changed how?"

"She wasn't herself," Lorelei says. "She acted drunk and young. And *stupid*. She didn't act that way when she *was* young and stupid."

"Selfish," Breena adds. "Like a kid who doesn't want to share her toys. And I did *not* like the vibes coming off that thing when I picked it up."

"Me, either," Lorelei agrees. "It was beyond creepy. It was...*malicious*."

I reach for it and frown when I feel absolutely nothing. "The stone is clean."

"No way." Lorelei takes it from me and blinks rapidly. "You're right. I don't feel anything at all now."

"I don't want to touch it," Breena says, shaking her head. "I'll take your word for it."

"How could it feel so sinister, so *awful* just a few moments ago and like nothing at all now?" Lorelei demands. "What in the goddess's name is going on here?"

I brush my hand down my face, trying to think clearly, but all I can see in my mind is Lucy, retching and crying.

I couldn't even reach her telepathically when I ran back here from Astrid and Hilda's house. I'd never been so damn frustrated.

"Something was attached to it," I say as Lorelei sets the cracked crystal on the table. "And it transferred itself to Lucy. How it got in, I don't know."

"I do," Breena insists. Her voice is thin with fear. "Lucy brought it in herself. By bringing the box inside, she *invited* whatever that was to come inside with it. It must have attached itself somehow."

"It could still be here," Lorelei says. "We have to cleanse the whole house. Sage and palo santo."

"I think we should use the singing bowl, too," Breena adds. "We need to put all of our tools to work here."

"I know where Lucy keeps her cleansing tools," I offer to the others. "Let's get to work."

Lorelei chooses a fresh bundle of sage and rosemary and a stick of palo santo from the shop and uses Lucy's personal bowl to hold the lit bundle and wood, beginning to work her way through the house, moving widdershins to banish.

Breena does the same with a bowl she holds on a pillow, using a thick wand to trace the rim, creating a beautiful noise.

Both women chant protection spells as they make

their way through the house toward the open door, ushering out anything bad.

I use my own methods.

Using an anointing oil that I mixed myself, I draw protection runes on all the windows and doors, also working counterclockwise after the women to keep out anything that's left after their smudging and sound healing.

When I reach Lucy's room, I also draw a rune on her forehead, being careful not to disturb her sleep.

Then I do the same for Nera.

Evil will attack a witch's familiar, especially when the only purpose is to cause pain.

And something was doing its best to harm Lucy tonight. I wish I could bring my coven in to help me with this. To surround the house with the circle and cast out anything that may wish her harm.

But for now, I have Breena and Lorelei, two powerful beings in their own right, to help me keep the woman I love safe.

When we've combed through every inch of the house and closed out anything we swept away, we return to the kitchen.

"I'm going to set new wards." Breena cleanses a bowl. "I know it's best when a witch sets her own wards for her home, but this will have to do for now until Lucy is strong enough to do it herself."

"She won't mind," Lorelei says, agreeing with her

cousin. "In fact, if it were me, I'd be mad if we *didn't* do this."

"Agreed," Breena concurs. "I'm going to set a protection simmer pot on the stove, as well. I know it's a *lot* of protection in this house tonight, but—"

"Under the circumstances, I'd say there can't be too much," I assure her and pat her shoulder. "Not tonight. Do what you need to do. I'm grateful."

Breena smiles sweetly and then gets to work on her simmer pot.

"It's convenient to work in a green witch's kitchen," Lorelei says thoughtfully as she pulls herbs and flowers out of containers for the spell she's working. "She literally has everything a witch could need. Oh, she even has calendula. That's not easy to find, but then again, if someone's going to have some, it's our Lucy."

"I called my mom when you were upstairs, Jonas. She and Astrid are working some magic of their own tonight to help us."

"Thank you."

I sit in a chair and drag my hand through my hair, suddenly more exhausted than I remember being in a long, long time.

"Part of me is surprised," Lorelei says, and I glance up to find her watching me, her eyes filled with speculation.

"About what?"

"Well, it's still really early in your relationship. Like, it's a baby romance. But it's not all sex and fluff. I saw that tonight with all this creepy shit going on. It's so much deeper than that between the two of you."

"There has been sex and fluff." I grin at the words. "But we're not children, Lorelei. If you're asking whether or not I'm in love with your cousin, I don't think there's any question that I am. I enjoy her. I'm completely fascinated by her. And I worry for her because something—or someone—is trying to hurt her. I won't let that happen."

We all turn our heads at the sound of Nera's whimper. Standing next to him is Lucy.

"You're awake," Breena says with surprise.

"Come." I take her hand and kiss it, searching her face. Her eyes still look tired, and she's lost all the color in her cheeks. Still, I can see that it's *Lucy* standing here with us. "Sit down."

"I'll make some tea," Breena announces and gets to work.

"Peppermint, please." Lucy swallows hard. "I'm still nauseated. What happened?"

"I was hoping you'd be able to tell us," I say as I sit next to her and tuck her hair behind her ear. "What do you remember?"

"I felt so odd." She swallows hard, and Nera lays his head in her lap. She strokes his long ears as she continues talking. "I wanted to celebrate. To be carefree and silly. And it was an addictive feeling, which is so odd. I don't like to drink too much, and I've never done any kind of mind-altering drugs because I'm afraid of what my magic would do under the influence of something."

"Not to mention, you *hate* wine, and you might have given your right ovary for a bottle of good red tonight," Lorelei says.

"Yeah, what's up with that?" Lucy asks, shaking her head. She smiles gratefully at Breena and accepts the cup of tea her cousin offers her. "I definitely wasn't in control of what was going on. And then, all I could do was cry and throw up."

"Do you think that whatever possessed you left at that time, and the sickness was your body's reaction to the possession?" Breena asks.

"I wasn't *possessed*," Lucy replies.

"Then what do you think it was?" I ask her and make her look into my eyes. "How would you explain it?"

"Maybe I ate something bad," she says, thinking it over. "It could have been a weird reaction to something."

"You're not allergic to anything that grows," Breena insists. "And we all ate the same things. It came in on that." She points at the broken agate.

Lucy's face pales even more when she looks at the crystal, and then she's on her feet and backing quickly away from it.

"Get that out of here."

The fear is palpable as Lorelei takes the crystal and hurries out the back door with it. I watch through the window as she takes it through the garden, out the gate, and into the trees.

"Honey," Breena says, rubbing Lucy's back. "Something had you tonight. But don't worry, we laid so much protection on this place, literally *nothing* can get inside without your consent. It's so strong, you might even have to give *written* consent."

Lucy gives her a shaky smile. "Thank you. Thank you so much."

Lorelei comes back into the kitchen and washes her hands. "I took it halfway home. I'll take it the rest of the way when I go in a bit and dispose of it in the ocean. It won't ever bother you again, Lucy."

"Okay." Lucy takes a long, deep breath. "Okay."

"Oh, and by the way," Lorelei continues, "your mom is here, and she's not leaving you again until this whole mess is cleaned up. She says you can try to make her mad enough to storm out, but it won't work."

Lucy presses her lips together, and her eyes fill with tears.

"Good. I could use my mom right about now. But tell her to stay out of the bedroom, or she might see some stuff she'd rather not."

Lorelei laughs. "She says she'll give you your privacy."

"What was that?" Lucy asks, looking over at me.

"I didn't say anything, sweetheart."

She frowns, purses her lips, and swallows hard. "Oh, okay."

She's been doing that a lot, asking me or others to repeat themselves when nothing has been said. It makes me wonder what's tormenting her and what she's been hearing.

I absolutely *despise* that I can't do more to help her.

"I really am tired," Lucy decides and finishes her tea. "I think I'll go to bed for the night. I'm sorry that our fun girls' night went to hell in a handbasket."

"I had a great time until we opened that box," Breena assures and gives her a big hug. "Go sleep off the nasty. You'll feel better tomorrow."

"Okay." Lucy kisses her cousin's cheek. "Have a good night, you guys."

Lucy and Nera leave the room.

"We're going," Lorelei says. "You are to stick to her like glue."

I nod, and when the women are gone, I lock the door and set one last protection spell before climbing the steps to Lucy's room.

She's back in bed with Nera, and she's already asleep.

I slide into bed with them and pull Lucy close. I need the comfort of having her in my arms.

They're all hanging.

I'm walking in a forest, through the trees, and everyone I've ever known is hanging from the limbs with ropes tight around their necks.

I'm too late.

I search and search for Lucy, still hopeful that she was spared, but all I hear is silence. No one calls out for help.

All that's here is death.

I swear I hear footsteps behind me. Rustling in the

fallen leaves. A twig snapping underfoot.

But when I whirl around, no one's there.

"Hello?" I call out.

"Jonas!"

"Lucy?" I whip in the direction of her voice. "Lucy!"

"Jonas, help me!"

I'm running now, my lungs burning from exertion. But I can't get through the mass of hanging bodies. It just never ends.

Suddenly, something falls on me, tackling me to the ground.

I can't breathe under the weight of it.

"Bark!"

I struggle to sit up, but Nera's lying on my chest, his nose against mine.

"Nera?" I glance over, but Lucy's not in bed with me. "Where is she?"

He barks again and jumps off the bed, bouncing and eager for me to follow him. I step into my shoes and hurry down the steps to the first floor—and stop cold.

The entire apothecary shop has been destroyed—everything tossed from the shelves and spilled, shattered, or broken on the floor.

"Nera?"

I hear another bark from the kitchen and almost slip in the remnants of broken tincture bottles on my way across the room.

More destruction here. The wards Breena made have been thrown and smashed against the wall, along with the simmer pot. It looks like a child had a temper tantrum and broke all his toys.

And, standing at the open door, is Lucy. She's on the threshold, the door wide open, and she's simply staring outside, her hair fluttering in the cold breeze.

I rush to her, take her shoulders in my hands, and turn her to me. She's bloody from head to toe, and my stomach jerks as I wonder if it's her blood or if she struggled with an intruder.

"Lucy?" The white film covering the irises of her eyes makes me shudder. "Where are you going, honey?"

She doesn't blink. Her eyes don't focus on mine.

"To him."

Nera barks and dances beside me. He stares outside, then looks up at me and whines, but when *I* look, no one's there.

I don't see what he does.

I raise my hands high over my head and begin the first spell that comes to mind, sending flames into the outdoor fireplace and the oven here in the kitchen.

Calling on my element and the deities, I repeat the spell over and over until the wind dies, and Nera calms, whining as he nudges Lucy's hand with his face.

Lucy falls into a heap on the floor, and I finish the spell, then lift her and signal for Nera to follow me.

Without thinking twice, I walk with Lucy in my arms all the way to Astrid and Hilda's house.

Halfway there, the older witches are already running toward me. They're out of breath and look terrified.

"Something imprisoned us," Astrid says. "We couldn't get out of the house."

"She can't stay at her place," I add immediately as we hurry back to Astrid and Hilda's. "It's not safe."

"We were trying to get to her," Hilda replies, hurrying ahead to the cottage.

Without asking, I start a fire in the hearth and set Lucy on the couch.

"Whatever has its sights set on Lucy is strong," I say at last and look up at the women. "It blocked me from her mind and sent me into a nightmare while it terrorized Lucy in her own home. And all of that after we'd all set incredibly strong protection spells. I've never seen anything like it."

"Mama," Lucy whimpers on the couch and scrunches her face in grief. "Don't go again."

"Oh, honey," Hilda says and brushes her knuckles down Lucy's cheek. "Wake up, darling. Come on now."

Lucy's eyes flutter open. Much to my relief, they're no longer white and filmy, but they're full of so much sadness it tears at my heart.

"She's gone," she whispers.

"Did you dream about your mother's death again?" Astrid asks softly.

"No." Lucy shakes her head in despair. "She's *gone.* It took her soul this time, and it made me watch."

We're stunned into silence as Lucy hangs her head in her hands and begins to weep.

"We're not safe," she says. "We'll never be safe."

CHAPTER SEVENTEEN
LUCY

"Tell me what you saw," Jonas says as he kneels in front of me, wrapping his big, warm hands around mine. His palms are so warm, so soothing against my freezing skin. "Talk to us, Luciana."

"It showed me everything." My voice sounds like it's coming from a tunnel. "Taunting my mom, confusing her. She was so scared that something would happen to you two."

I glance up at the aunts and frown when I see them crying.

And Breena and Lorelei are here. When did they get here?

"So, she hid a lot from you because she was convinced that telling you too much would put you at risk." I swallow hard, dreading what I'm about to tell them next.

"What else?" Jonas's voice is gentle, but his eyes are intently focused on mine. I can see the worry and torment in his gaze and just want to hug him close and reassure him that I'm okay.

But I'm not entirely sure that's true.

"She was terrified," I continue. "And she tried *everything* she could think of to keep it at bay. But it was no use. It showed me every step, every moment of terror. And after it caught her—"

I shake my head, and Jonas sits next to me, rubbing my back and kissing my temple, sharing his strength with me. "Take your time."

I nod, brush at a tear, and continue. "It was pure torture for her. It was not an easy death at all. Not only was there physical pain, but it also promised her that it would come for me next, and explained in minute detail all the things it would put me through. She cried and begged for mercy for me, and it fucking *laughed* at her. And then, it killed her. She hung in her own living room until I found her the next morning."

"You *found* her?" Jonas asks me.

"I did." I glance at the other four women and feel their love for me coming at me in waves. "She fought and loved us all with everything she had—until the very end."

"Oh, baby, she still does," Astrid reminds me.

"I have a question." Jonas frowns. "You all have death wards. How did it kill her? It's obviously not mortal."

"The girls got the tattoos against their mothers' wishes," Hilda says, eyeing her daughter. "We didn't think it was appropriate. Not the tattoo itself, necessarily, but the ward. A witch should be able to use and alter any spell they cast. They should be able to change their mind. But the tattoos are permanent."

"We got them anyway," Lorelei says with a wink.

"The moms have different wards," Breena adds. "They have it woven into their hair each year on the summer solstice."

"It made my mom cut hers out." I press my lips together. "It told her that if she did, it would spare me. It was a lie, of course."

"I'm so sorry you had to see all of that," Breena says.

"That's not all I saw," I continue. "Tonight, in my house, it made me destroy *everything*. Everything in the shop is ruined. My kitchen is obliterated."

I feel my chest heave, and I bury my face in Nera's fur.

"It made me kick Nera."

I'm okay, Nera says and nuzzles against my neck. *I know you love me.*

"Oh, honey." Lorelei sits on my other side.

"And then my mom was there. Lorelei, you told me that she was staying in the house to watch over things. She was there. It showed her to me. She was fighting it, and then it killed her again. But this time, it was her soul. She's gone."

The last few words come out on a sob as I close my eyes, still leaning on Nera. I weep.

"She's not gone," Astrid insists.

"She is. I saw it happen. I'm just so angry."

"Lucy," Jonas says. "Open your eyes, sweetheart. She's not gone."

I lift my head. Standing right before me as if she were skin and bone is my mom. She smiles softly, her eyes churning with emotion.

I jump up and try to wrap my arms around her in a hug, but I pass right through her.

"I guess I got a little excited."

I turn to find Mom laughing, along with the others.

"How is this possible?" I demand.

"It was a nightmare," Hilda assures. "It was scaring you and doing a good job of it. But it didn't destroy your mother."

"Oh, thank the goddess." I want to reach for her so badly. I want her to hug me close, brush my hair back, and tell me that everything will be okay.

Even if it's a lie, I want to hear her say it.

"I'm so mad at you," I inform her, and she just smiles and shrugs. "I'm an adult now, Mom. You don't have to keep teaching me lessons."

"You'll always be my daughter," is all she says in reply, and her voice is music to my ears. "You'll stay here for a few days."

"No, I have a mess to clean up at home—"

"You'll stay here," Jonas interrupts and stands beside me. It's not lost on me that everyone steps away as if they're giving us a moment to ourselves. "It's not safe at your house, Lucy. I saw what it did to you, and I do not trust that it's gone. So, you'll go nowhere near it for the time being. We're only a week out from Samhain, and things are only going to ramp up."

"Jonas—"

"Please." He tips his forehead to mine and links our fingers at our sides. *You'll never know the terror I went through tonight. Don't make me relive it if we have a way of avoiding it.*

"Okay," I whisper, feeling exhausted. "I'll stay here. But where will you stay?"

"Why, here, of course," Astrid says. "Honey, we're not under any kind of illusion that the two of you don't sleep together."

"I *hope* they are," Hilda agrees.

"I guess it's decided, then," I reply and smile at Jonas. "We'll stay here for now. But you should go check on things in Hallows End."

"Eventually," is all he says.

"I'm bored out of my mind."

Neither Astrid nor Hilda acknowledges that I've said anything at all.

"Hello? I'm not invisible."

"No, dear, you're just annoying," Astrid replies as she works on her knitting. Hilda smiles but keeps her eyes down, focusing on the book she's reading. "And we love you, so we're keeping quiet."

"I'm going home."

I stand and march into the guest room where Jonas is also reading and prop my hands on my hips.

"I'm going home."

"I heard you," he says mildly and turns a page in his book.

"Great. It's decided, then." I grab the few things I have here that are mine, which isn't much because no one was willing to go to my house to gather anything for me. "Come, Nera."

"I didn't say you could actually go." Jonas's voice comes from behind me.

"I beg your pardon?" I turn slowly and narrow my eyes at the man I love.

"You heard me." He closes the book, sets it on the table next to him, and then rises.

"I do find it sexy when you're the alpha male," I admit, feeling my blood stir at the intensity of his gaze. "But I feel *great*, Jonas. And not weird-good like that night with the girls. I'm myself, my energy is back in spades, and I have things to do. I have to clean my shop and reopen it. It's my busiest time of year, and I'm losing out on money every day I stay closed."

"Do you think I'll risk you just because it's tourist season?"

His voice is too calm—on the verge of angry-calm.

"You're not risking me."

"Luciana—"

"I can't just hide here." I walk to him, pressing myself

against him. "It's my *home*. My business, Jonas. If there's any funny business, we'll come right back here, but I'm telling you, I have to get out of here and do something. I've already texted Delia, and she's going to meet me at the shop so we can start cleaning up."

"How much does Delia know?" he asks me.

"She's a member of the coven and my sole employee. I trust her. For the love of Freya, Jonas, the whole coven knows what happened."

"As they should."

"What are you worried about?"

He buries his nose in my hair and takes a long, deep breath. "That it'll use one of them to get to you, and we won't know it because it's someone we trust."

"It's okay." I lean back far enough to cup his face in my hands. "I promise you, it's going to be okay."

"Don't do that." He takes one of my hands and kisses the palm. "Don't promise something you don't know for sure will happen."

"I *can* promise that," I insist. "Let's go to the shop and dig in. And, as I said, if something is off, we'll come back here."

"We're all going with you."

I turn to find the aunts watching from the doorway, holding their brooms.

"I think I can use all the help I can get."

Delia is waiting when we arrive, sitting on the top step of the shop's porch.

"I hope you haven't been waiting long," I say as I

stand on the sidewalk and gaze up at the old, puritan-style home I bought several years ago with the express intention of using it as my home *and* business.

And now, I'm half-afraid to go inside.

But, with Jonas at my side, along with my aunts and cousins, I lift my chin and walk up the steps to meet Delia.

"You okay?" she murmurs as she hugs me.

"I'm *fantastic*." I smile and then approach the door, keying in the code for the locks before opening it wide. "We're going to leave this door open, along with the windows, while we clean. I'm warning anything inside that shouldn't be, you'll want to take your leave. Now. I'm done being fucked with."

"We didn't raise our girls to be timid." Astrid smiles proudly. "Come on, witches, we have work to do."

Jonas doesn't leave my side for a moment all afternoon, and it helps to soothe my frayed nerves to have him close by. We sweep, clean, and laugh the afternoon away, and then, once all the trash has been taken out, we restock the shop's shelves, and I go out into the garden to pick some fresh herbs for the ovens.

All the while, the property feels calm.

It feels *clean*.

The cold nights have begun to kill off some of the plants for the season, so I trim things back and prepare it for winter before walking into the greenhouse, smiling at the sight of all of the *green*.

"Hello, pretties."

As usual, the leaves all seem to sit up as if to say hello.

For the next fifteen minutes, I tend the plants in the greenhouse, pick some flowers, and nudge the calendula along with the wiggle of my fingers.

"There you are," Breena says from the doorway. "You always did like wandering off to play with your plants."

"It soothes me."

"I know. Everything's pretty much done inside. I think we're all going to head out now."

"Oh, I'll come in and thank everyone."

I grab my already full basket and walk with Breena inside, where everyone is gathered in the kitchen.

"I just can't thank you enough for helping me today."

"There was nowhere else we'd be." Delia checks the time. "But I do have a hot date, so I'll see you tomorrow."

"See you!"

I'm hugged and kissed, and Hilda makes me promise to call if I need anything before they all leave Jonas and me with Nera. I sit, listening to the stillness of the house.

"There's nothing here." I sigh and look up into Jonas's blue eyes. "Whatever was here before is gone now. I don't know how I know, I just do."

"I agree." He drags his knuckles down my cheek. "And I'm glad for it."

"Do you know what we need?" I raise my eyebrow and feel a sassy smile spread over my mouth.

"I couldn't begin to guess."

"A bath. A nice, long soak in the tub. And I just mixed up a new bath tea for us, too."

"We certainly can't let something that special go to waste." He kisses my hand. I *love* how this man can't keep his hands or lips off me. "Let's go."

I don't ask Nera to stay behind when we go upstairs. I can still sense the fear and uncertainty in him, and I want him nearby, so he follows us up to the owner's suite and lies on his bed.

"He's as exhausted as we are."

Jonas looks down at my familiar with affection. "He should be. It's been a busy week."

I run the water in the tub and drop the mesh bag that holds all the herbs and flowers for the bath under the stream, turning as Jonas grips the hem of my shirt and tugs it over my head, letting it fall to the floor.

With greedy eyes, he waves a hand, bringing all the candles in the room to life, and then he finishes undressing me.

When I'm naked and standing in the candlelight, his eyes slowly make the journey from my feet to my face, and then he takes in a long, deep breath.

"My goddess, you're beautiful."

I wrinkle my nose, ready to come back with something witty, but he shakes his head sharply.

"You *are* beautiful, Luciana. In every way."

"And you're still clothed."

He narrows his eyes and quickly tugs out of his clothes, then helps me into the hot bath.

I lean back on one side, and Jonas does the same on the other so we can face each other.

He lifts one of my feet and begins digging his thumb into the arch, sending me straight to ecstasy.

"One thing hasn't changed through the ages," he says mildly.

"What's that?"

"Women *love* a foot rub."

"Oh?" I tilt my head to the side, watching him. "I was under the impression that you haven't been intimate with a woman in more than three hundred years."

"That's true," he replies and moves his hand down to knead the heel of my foot. "That's absolutely true. But I do read and pay attention, and women enjoy a good foot rub."

I close my eyes and tip my head back against the rim of the tub, taking in the fragrance of the lavender and roses, the heat of the water, and the feel of Jonas against me, his hands doing wonderful things to my feet.

"You're not wrong. Goddess, I love you."

His hands still long enough that I open my eyes, only to find him frowning down into the water.

"What's wrong?"

He shakes his head and starts rubbing my foot again, but I pull it from his grasp and move through the water to loop my arms around his neck.

"What's wrong?" I ask again.

"There are moments, such as these," he begins and twirls a wet lock of my hair around his index finger, "that

I'm reminded just how deeply I love you and how absolutely terrified I am at the same time."

"What are you afraid of?"

"Losing you, of course." His eyes are on the lock of hair around his finger. "I can't ask you to marry me, to truly *claim* you as mine, until we resolve the mess of the curse and find a witch murderer."

"Why not?"

The question seems to trip him up. "What do you mean, why not?"

"Why can't you ask me to marry you? Why can't you *claim* me?"

"Because when all is said and done, we may not be able to be together, Lucy. If we don't lift the curse, I'll be gone, and you'll forget all about me."

I shake my head as I straddle his lap and slowly take him inside me. His hands instinctively glide up my back. Once I'm seated on him, I take his face in my hands once more.

"I want you to understand something, Jonas Morley. Whether it's for a day or a hundred years, I *am* yours, and there is nothing that could ever happen that would make me forget you. I carry your mark."

I show him my hand and smile when he leans forward to kiss it.

"We belong to each other, my love." I kiss his lips tenderly as he cups my ass in his big hands and urges me to move. "I'm yours until I take my last breath."

His muscles bunch beneath my hands as the water

sluices around us, and when we go over together, he presses his lips to mine as if memorizing me.

"Mine," he whispers between gasps for breath, and I smile against him.

"Mine," I agree softly.

"Let's make it official," he says and then laughs. "I know that's not the most romantic of proposals, but I don't want to wait. Marry me, Luciana."

"Tonight."

His eyebrows climb into his dark hair, but his eyes are full of humor.

"That's a bit quick to organize a wedding."

"I don't need the pomp and circumstance. At least not right now. We can perform our own handfasting ceremony together and bind our souls. We don't need witnesses for that."

He brushes his fingertips down my sternum and over my heart.

"Do you think your cousins will let you live another day if you don't invite them to be here for such an occasion?"

I bite my lip and then let out a little laugh.

"I'll call them over. But I want it done tonight, Jonas."

His expression sobers, and he pulls me in for another long, slow kiss.

"Then it'll be tonight."

Chapter Eighteen
Jonas

"I'm sorry if you were all sleeping peacefully. Kind of," Lucy says to her aunts and cousins with a sweet smile lighting her gorgeous face. She radiates with excitement and joy, and it's a nice change after all the fear and grief lately. "But I'm only a little sorry."

"Are you kidding?" Breena jumps up and down in excitement, fiddling with a bouquet. "Who needs sleep when one of your favorite people is getting *married*?"

"The coven will want to throw you a big party," Astrid reminds her but pulls her in close for a hug. "And you know that we wouldn't miss this for anything. Of all our girls, you *were* the most likely to want to do this on a whim and in the dark."

"It's almost midnight," Hilda says as she sets one final white candle on her picnic table.

I wave my hand, and all the wicks light, making the girls smile.

We decided to do this in the aunts' garden.

"I'm sorry that your coven isn't here with you," Lucy says as she takes my hand. "I know you care about many people in Hallows End and wish they could be here for this."

I kiss her forehead and take a long, deep breath. "One day, they'll know. We'll celebrate with them then."

"It'll just be a long string of parties," Lorelei adds with a smile. "As it should be."

"I've kept this for you." Hilda steps forward, holding a braided leather strap in her hands. "This was the cord that your parents used for their ceremony, and I know that your mom wants you to use it for yours."

"I can still see her," Lucy says with a watery smile, looking over Hilda's shoulder. "And I'm glad because I'd be *really* mad if she left during this part. Thank you for saving it for me. I'll keep it safe for, well...later."

I want babies, Jonas Morley. Lots of babies.

I smile, my heart skipping at the thought. I'd come to the realization long ago that I would never be a husband or a father. It was something I had to grieve and move past. And I had.

But now, it's within my grasp.

I will marry Lucy tonight and promise to love her for as long as I exist.

I just hope that existence is long enough to give her the children she craves.

Let's start with this. We'll add babies later.

She snorts. We move into position under the bright,

star-filled sky lit by the glow of the almost full moon and pledge ourselves to each other.

"Let's begin."

"**X**ander."

My head comes up at the man's name, and I see that he's just walked through the door of Lucy's apothecary. Lucy walks to him and offers him a hug, but he skims the room, his eyes narrowed and calculating.

When he sees me, he walks over and shakes my hand.

"What are you looking for?" I ask him quietly so as not to disturb the customers browsing in the shop.

"Just checking the energy," he replies. "It seems calm."

"There's been nothing since we returned last night," I confirm, still amazed that it was only yesterday that we came back to clean, and less than twelve hours since Lucy and I were handfasted. I'm a married man.

"Good. Congratulations." He shakes my hand with a smile. "I have so many questions, but those can wait for a later time."

"I suspect we have some of the same ones," I reply. "But I love her. She's meant for me."

"She is. For better or worse. And I have something for you."

He reaches into his pocket and pulls out a simple black velvet box.

"I know this isn't the original box it came in, but what's inside is pretty damn old. Open it."

I flip the top and feel emotion roll through me. "This was my mother's ring."

It's a gold band with a single simply set ruby. I haven't seen it in centuries. And when I take it out of the box, I can feel my mother's essence in it.

"It's been passed down and was given to me, but it should be yours, Jonas."

"If it was given to you, you should keep it."

"No," he insists. "She was your *mother*. You knew and loved her. She's merely a story to me. There's a big difference. Besides, when my time comes, the woman I love is an aquamarine girl."

I smile and look back down at the ring sitting on my index finger. "I'm grateful, Xander."

"And you're welcome. We need to get together soon. All of us. I received a call from Miss Sophia the other night when she couldn't reach Lucy. It's nothing urgent, but it's information we didn't have before."

"We will see you soon, then."

"Have a good day."

He stops to talk with Lucy for a moment on his way out, and then he's gone.

I can't stop staring at the gift he gave me. I had thought this lost long ago, and it astounds me that it wasn't.

"What did Xander want?" Lucy asks after escorting a customer out. "You two had your heads together."

I look into her eyes and grin as I tuck the ring away. I may not have proposed with great finesse last night, but I plan to do better when I present her with the ring.

"He'd like for us to get together soon so he can share some information, and he wanted to congratulate us."

"Yeah, he said so when he stopped by me, as well. That's nice of him. I feel kind of bad that I didn't invite him to join us last night since he's been a part of my life for a really long time. But I didn't want to make Lorelei uncomfortable."

"I think he understands that it was just family and spur-of-the-moment."

"You're right." She grins and presses her lips to mine. "My husband is so smart."

"Is that so?"

She's still chuckling when someone clears their throat behind her.

"How can I help you?" she asks as she turns.

"I need something to help me sleep," the young woman says. "I'm in college, and my classes have me so stressed out that I have insomnia."

"I have just the thing for you," Lucy assures her as they take off to discuss the woman's options.

I haven't let Lucy out of my sight all day. While I don't feel anything sinister here, and I *do* think she's safe, I won't take any chances.

After she collects the money for the bedtime tea she

just sold, Lucy turns to Delia. "I have to run into the kitchen to check on some things. Can you handle this for fifteen minutes?"

"Of course," Delia assures her. "I'll call if it gets too busy."

"Thanks." With a grateful smile, Lucy walks through the doorway to the kitchen, and I follow behind her, ready to relocate to the kitchen table, under which Nera snores loudly.

He's slept all day, likely still recovering from all the activities of late.

Lucy turns quickly, bumps into my chest, and then takes a deep breath.

"Okay. I love you."

"And I love you."

"And I think it's really, really sweet that you're watching over me because you feel that you need to protect me."

"I *do* need to protect you."

"Jonas, you're hovering."

I raise an eyebrow. "I beg your pardon?"

"You're *hovering*. I need you to take a breath for a bit. You've been glued to me for almost a week. I'm not complaining. I appreciate you so, so much—"

"I know." I brush a strand of her bright red hair off her cheek.

"But it's just...I'm safe. I have Delia and a whole store full of people. Nera's here. I promise not to leave the building to go to my garden or anywhere else. *Please*, go take a break. You really need to go into Hallows End, Jonas. You haven't been back in almost a week."

"Absolutely not."

"Jonas." She takes my hand and presses my palm to her cheek. "Those people still need you. After things changed with the baby being born, you need to check on them more than ever. Just in case."

I take a deep breath and feel frustration bubble within me. I know she's right, but I hate the idea of being too far away from her.

What if I can't reach you like this again?

I'm here. We're stronger than ever, Jonas.

I nod, kiss her forehead, and then her lips. "I know that I need to go back to check in with them. I'm going to make the rounds, make sure that everything is as it should be, and then I'm coming right back."

"I think that sounds like a good idea." She kisses my lips with a loud, happy smack. "Have a good walk."

Nera wakes as I open the back door to the garden. I point at him and then at his mistress.

"Keep watch."

He sits up, coming to attention, and I nod in approval.

"Good boy. I'll see you both soon."

The walk into the woods and over the bridge is one I could do with my eyes closed. As usual, my clothes change as I cross the small bridge, along with the weather.

I step from late autumn sunshine into a cold drizzle.

I shouldn't have stayed away from Hallows End for as long as I did. I *do* have responsibilities here that I can't ignore, even if Lucy is the priority.

Did you get there okay? I hear her ask in my mind, and I'm relieved to know that the tether hasn't been blocked.

Yes, just entering my cabin now. I'll make sure everything is good here before I walk through the village.

I walk inside, and everything is as I left it after the baby's birth last week.

Good. All is well here, too.

I gather some things from my desk and shelves to take back to Lucy's with me when I go, set everything on the chair by the front door to pick up on my way by later, and then set off through town.

At first, everything seems normal. It's halfway through the month, and it looks like it always does at this time during the cycle.

But when I get to Louisa's cottage, I frown. She's not out front tending to her garden as she always is, even when there's rain. In fact, it doesn't look like anything has been tended in a few days.

That's *not* normal, so I walk to the front door and knock.

Louisa's husband, John, answers the door, looking exhausted and worried.

"Jonas, thank the goddess."

"Is something wrong with Louisa?" I step inside and look through the doorway to the bedroom where Louisa lies in bed.

"She is ill," John says and swallows hard. "Fever, chills. She will not eat or drink any water. She seems to see things that are not there at all."

"May I?"

"Yes, please."

I hurry to Louisa's side and take her hand as I press my other hand to her head.

"Her fever is high," I mutter. "Louisa, 'tis Jonas."

She doesn't stir at my words, and I look back at John, who only frowns and looks helpless.

"How long has she been like this?"

"Three days," he replies. "And it is not just my Louisa. Several other members of the coven are in the same condition."

"How many others?"

"I do not know for sure. I have stayed here to tend to her. Jonas, what kind of illness is making its way through Hallows End?"

"I do not know for sure." I press my lips together, trying to think. I know there are herbs I can use to help with the fever, but modern medicine would be so much better.

Come get some Tylenol.

I shake my head at Lucy's request in my mind. *I don't think I can bring it back here. Just like my clothes change, it will be taken from me.*

You have to try, she insists. *I'll have everything you need waiting for you at the bridge. I know you don't want me to come there, so I won't, but you have to try to bring the medicine to them. They won't remember this in two weeks, Jonas.*

She's right.

"I'm going to go get some medicine," I inform John. "She will need clean water to drink."

"I will fetch it," John promises as I hurry out of his house and make the rounds to the other members of the coven.

Every household has someone gravely ill, including young children.

Guilt sits heavy in my stomach as I cross the bridge. There's a basket waiting for me, and without even looking inside, I pick it up and cross back over.

To my utter shock, the basket and its contents make it over with me.

I run to Louisa and John's and offer her two Tylenol first.

"What is *that*?" John asks, staring at the plastic bottle in my hand.

"It's medicine," I reply and urge Louisa to drink the water to wash down the two capsules. "It will help with her fever. We have to get it lowered."

I use a digital thermometer against her forehead to get a reading.

"It's much too high."

"Jonas, where did you get all of this?" John asks, concern thick in his voice. "I've never seen anything like this before."

"I know." I look into the other man's eyes. "I cannot

explain it to you, but I assure you that this will help her. I will not do anything to harm your wife."

He wipes his hand over his mouth and then looks down at Louisa.

"I know you would not harm her. But later, I want to know what is going on."

"I will tell you whatever I am able to," I assure him. When I'm done with the medicine, I repack the basket and stand. "I will be back to give her another dose later. I have to go to the other homes and help them, as well."

"Go," he urges. "Help them. And thank you, Jonas."

"You are welcome."

I move from home to home, answering similar questions about what I have with me and how it came to be in my possession. But my coven trusts me, and they don't press when I evade the questions as best I can.

When I leave the last house, I hurry back over the bridge to Lucy's so I can restock the medicine and check in with her.

"Jonas," Lucy says and hurries to me, pulling me in to hold me close. "My goddess, what is going on?"

"I don't know." I accept the water she offers and take a long drink to soothe my dry throat. "They're *so* sick. I don't know what kind of virus it is, but it's caused a bad fever. Some have rashes from it. I need more supplies."

"I had more delivered." She passes me two bags filled with more medicine, teas, honey, and everything else they could need. "You have to stay with them for a while, Jonas. You know it's the right thing to do."

"I don't want to leave you here alone."

"Nera and I will sleep at Breena's," she assures me. "I don't want you to worry at all, and if I stay here, that's what will happen. We will be fine with Breena."

I breathe a sigh of relief and rest my forehead against hers.

Thank you. I'm sorry this is happening.

"You don't have anything to be sorry for." She wraps her sweet arms around me to hug me tightly. "Something is fucking with all of us. In both times. It pisses me off, Jonas."

"You and me both, my love." I kiss her cheek. "I have to go back. It's almost time to start handing out medicine again. And I need to see if it's helping with the fevers and such."

"I really should come and help you," she says.

"I'd rather you stay here," I reply. "Not that I don't want or need your help, but something in my gut tells me you're safer here."

"I'm in the habit of listening to gut instincts," she says with a nod. "But, seriously, if you need *anything* else, just say so, and I'll bring it to you."

"Thank you." I pull her against me and kiss her long and slow. "That will have to tide us over for a little while."

She presses her lips together and then licks them, seeming to savor my taste.

"Mm." She smiles when I narrow my eyes at her. "Go take care of them. I'll be here when you're done."

I kiss her one last time before taking the bags and walking back to the bridge.

I'm relieved when, once again, the medicines and bags make it through with me, and then I hurry right over to Louisa's house. John immediately lets me in and blows out a breath.

"How is she?"

"A little better," he says. "But she keeps talking about a curse and how we have to lift it. She's making no sense."

Actually, she makes excellent sense.

I hurry to her and see that Louisa is sitting up in bed, but she's definitely weak—her head lolls back and forth. When she sees me, she reaches her hand out for me.

"Jonas."

"I am here, my friend." I take her hand and kiss her fingers. "Is the medicine helping?"

"A little. Jonas, we have to lift the curse."

My heart leaps at her words. How is it possible that she remembers?

"How do we do that, Louisa?"

Her eyes fill with tears. "With a sacrifice."

CHAPTER NINETEEN
LUCY

"I absolutely *love* these shells," I say as I drag my fingertips over a massive shell sitting on Lorelei's coffee table. "Where did you find them? I've never seen anything like this on our shoreline."

Lorelei grins and passes me a plate of crab cakes that she just pulled out of the oven. "You just don't know where to look."

"No," Breena disagrees and bites into a cake. "They just magically show up for you, Lorelei."

"It's the whole sea witch thing," I say and share a bite with Nera. "Thanks for dinner, by the way."

"No problem. I have chocolate cake for dessert. It has sprinkles and everything."

"Are you sick?" Breena demands. "Because you're not usually one to cook much. Or, you know, at all."

"I took a cooking class in LA," she informs us and pulls her legs up under her on the sofa. "I got bored a lot because I didn't know anyone and I'm not great at making new friends. So, I found ways to occupy my time. The cooking class was my favorite. I hardly ever burn toast anymore."

"What's your favorite thing to cook?" I ask her.

"I didn't say I *like* to cook," she clarifies, waving her fork in the air. "I just said it was my favorite class. However, I don't mind baking. I actually like *that* a lot. I think this cake turned out good."

"I think the crab cakes are delicious," I say and take the last bite. "But I always have room for chocolate cake. Also, how are things between you and Xander?"

Lorelei scowls at me over her fork. "Why do we have to talk about him? We were having such a lovely time."

"Because when you two are in the same vicinity, the air is electric, and we're nosy," Breena says and takes a delicate bite of her crab cake.

"Aside from seeing him when we all get together, I don't see him at all." She sighs and then looks up. "Wait. That's not true. Sometimes, I see him flying overhead as a raven, and I've seen him on the beach as a black cat."

"Isn't that sweet?" I ask. "He's looking out for you."

"I think *he's* the nosy one," Lorelei says, her tone as dry as the Sahara.

"You could just come right out and tell him to leave you alone," I suggest, but Lorelei just sighs.

"No, I can't. Because *then* he'll know that he gets to me, and I won't give him the satisfaction."

"So adult of you." I laugh behind my glass of water as

Lorelei's glare shoots daggers at me from across the room. "What? You know it's true. Just have an adult conversation with him."

"I don't think so," she says. "Anyway, how is married life?"

"Great, but we're already spending the night apart, what with this new weird illness making its way through Hallows End."

"How are they doing?" Breena asks.

"Jonas reached out just before we came over here for dinner and said the fever is starting to subside, thanks to the Tylenol."

"I guess it's good they'll all forget soon. Otherwise, they'd be confused as hell," Lorelei says. "Unless we manage to lift the curse, in which case, we'll just have to explain things to them."

"I wonder what's triggering the illness," Breena questions. "And all the weird changes—changes that aren't exactly *good* ones."

"Who knows? What with *all* of the weird stuff happening lately..." I take our empty plates to the kitchen and load them into the dishwasher. "It could be anything, and my brain is just too tired to try to figure it out."

"It's all just creepy," Lorelei decides as she and Breena join me in the kitchen. Lorelei pulls a long knife out of her drawer and cuts into the cake. "I'm ready for Salem to get back to its *normal* creepy. We don't need all the extra stuff."

"Agreed," I say and accept a piece of cake, taking a bite. "Mm, this is really good."

"*So* good," Breena agrees.

"Thanks." Lorelei takes a bite herself, and the power goes out. I hear Nera whimper in the living room.

It's okay, I assure him, but he hurries over to my side and leans against my leg.

"The wind has been blowing all day," Lorelei says with a frown. "I was afraid I'd lose power."

Suddenly, the lights all come back on, and my cousin smiles.

"Good thing I bought a generator."

"Good idea," I say with a nod. "I remember Aunt Astrid complaining about losing power here a lot."

"It happens often with the high winds coming off the ocean," Lorelei replies. "So, I thought it was a good idea to have this installed. It's hooked up to the natural gas, so I don't even have to worry about filling or replacing a gas tank."

"Handy," Breena says with an approving nod as the wind howls outside. "Maybe we should head back to my house in case I've lost power there, too?"

"We should check on it," I agree. "But will you be okay here, Lorelei?"

"Of course. Storms are my jam, and I have a little magic to work tonight. But, yeah, get home before it gets too bad out there. Let me know that you got home safely."

Moments later, Breena, Nera, and I are walking the

short distance to Breena's house. As soon as we cross the street from Lorelei's cottage, the wind dies.

There is no storm.

It's completely still.

"It's so weird how the wind pattern is different on the shoreline," Breena says, but we pick up our pace.

Nera won't leave my side, and the fur on the back of his neck is up.

"I don't like this," I whisper. "From now on, we drive."

"I'm with you on that," Breena says, and we move even faster when her house comes into view. Once safely inside, Breena locks the door, and we turn to stare at each other. "I wasn't the only one who got the creeps, right?"

"No, you weren't. Nera and I felt it, too."

Breena sinks onto a chair and drops her face into her hands. "I'm going to be honest with you here, Luce. I'm terrified. I'm not equipped to deal with stuff like this."

"You're a powerful woman," I reply, shaking my head, but she stands and paces the room.

"I know that I'm a strong *witch*," she says. "I know my Craft, and I'm learning more all the time. But, Lucy, this is so much more than that. I am not a strong enough woman to deal with this much fear and uncertainty. I hate it so much."

"I'm sorry." I pull her in for a hug and rock us both back and forth. "I know that your heart can't take this kind of stuff, and I'm sorry. But we'll have to agree to disagree, because I think you *are* strong enough to handle literally anything."

She sighs and pulls back from me. "I want it all to be over."

"Me, too."

I call Lorelei to let her know we're safe while Breena takes a hot shower. Then, with Nera always staying close, I take a nice, hot shower of my own and get ready for bed.

It's a little early yet, but I'm exhausted from the past week of events, and we were all up late last night with the handfasting ceremony.

Did we really get married just last night?

I can almost see Jonas's smile as he hears my thought.

How are you, sweetheart?

Just fine. Nera and I are with Breena, getting ready for bed. I'm tired. How are things there?

Nera jumps onto the bed with me, and we curl up together with my iPad. I like to watch videos on YouTube about gardening and herbalism before bed.

Beginning to calm down. I'll stay through the night, just to make sure that everything is okay, and then I'll head your way in the morning.

Good. I miss you. Get some rest, if you can.

You rest, my love. I'll see you soon.

Love you.

I cozy down with Nera, and before I can even turn on the tablet, I drift off to sleep.

The bed is jostled, and I wake to find Breena slipping under the covers.

"I need you," she says, her voice shaking.

"I'm here." I open my arms, and she wraps herself around me, shivering as badly as her voice. "Hey, what's going on? Talk to me, Breen."

Nera lays his big head on her side and watches with worried brown eyes as Breena clings to me in the moonlight.

"Bad dream," she whispers. "Really bad."

"It's okay," I assure her, rubbing her back. I kiss her wet cheek. "It's okay, honey."

"Oh, goddess, Lucy." Her voice catches.

"Do you want to tell me about it?"

"Absolutely not."

I hold her close and pat Nera's head, comforting them both until we all fall asleep.

"You spoil us," I announce as I pop more pancake into my mouth. Lorelei came over first thing this morning by car, and Breena's been stuffing us full of her special pancakes, bacon and homemade mochas.

It's the *best*.

"I love that you're so nurturing," Lorelei adds. "You're going to be an awesome mom someday."

Breena snorts, but I see the small, satisfied smile on her lips as she turns back to the stove so she can flip the pancakes.

"There's no secret to these," she says. "I just add a little extra vanilla and a bit of cinnamon."

"And a lot of love," I continue. "Maybe some eye of newt."

That makes her laugh. "I can't help that I like to take care of the people I love. I've always been this way. I like to cook for you, sew, make you things."

"Acts of service is your love language," I inform her. "In spades."

"What's your love language?" Lorelei asks me.

"Hmm." I take a bite of bacon. "Maybe physical touch. I've always been a hugger. What about you?"

"I think it's quality time," she says after pondering it for a minute. Suddenly, someone knocks on the door.

"I'll get it." I stand. "You keep making pancakes."

I walk to the door, surprised when I see Giles standing on the other side of it.

"Hey," I say as I pull open the door but then pause. "Wait. Say something that only the *real* Giles would know."

It doesn't make him laugh. "Where is she?"

He brushes past me, a man on a mission.

"Come on in," I mutter and close the door behind him.

Giles scans the room, his eyes narrow, and when he spots Breena in the kitchen, he rushes to her, turns her to him, and yanks her into his arms.

"Fucking hell." His voice shakes, similarly to the way hers did last night.

Breena's hands come up to awkwardly pat his back.

"Um, hi. Are you okay?"

His face is buried in her neck now, and he's holding on for dear life. I can see that he's trembling.

Lorelei and I share a look.

"No," Giles says at last, answering her. "I'm not okay at all. Gods, I watched you die."

"What?" Lorelei stands, and the three of us stare at him as he reluctantly pulls away from Breena and starts pacing the floor.

"In my dream last night, I watched you fucking *die*, and I couldn't stop it. I couldn't do anything about it. Every time I ran toward you, something slammed me back. Blocked me. And you were screaming, reaching out for me."

He wipes a shaking hand over his mouth.

"You were reaching for me," he says again and clears his throat. He looks terrified, pale and hollow-eyed. "And you kept screaming for me to help you, and I just *couldn't*. Stars, I've never felt so damn worthless."

"I'm okay," Breena assures him and reaches for his hand, giving it a squeeze.

Lorelei and I share another look.

"But I had the same dream."

Giles's face whips up to hers. "You did?"

"Yes, and it terrified me."

"She crawled into bed with Nera and me," I confirm. Nera raises his head at the mention of his name.

Giles wraps his arms around Breena again, holding her close. "I wish you'd come to *me.*"

Breena's wide, green eyes find ours, and she mouths, *Why would I?*

Lorelei rolls her eyes.

"Okay, loverboy," Lorelei says. "Sit, eat some of the best pancakes you've ever had, and let's all calm down."

"I haven't been calm since about two this morning." He lets Breena go and paces to the window to look out at the backyard. "It was *real.* There was nothing dreamlike about it."

Breena doesn't say anything, she just flips the pancakes and begins brewing up a mocha for Giles.

"It *was* a dream," Breena says at last in her sweet way. "Giles, I'm right here, and although I had the same dream, it wasn't real."

He shakes his head but sits at the table and takes a bite of a pancake, then his stunned eyes lift to Breena's.

"Holy shit, Breena."

"What's wrong?" Lorelei asks.

"This *is* the best pancake I've ever eaten."

"Told you," Lorelei says smugly. "Breena's an ace in the kitchen. And just wait until you get that mocha."

"You don't have to sell him on her," I mutter, ready to start giggling as Breena sets the mug in front of Giles and then returns to her seat to continue eating her own breakfast.

"I didn't mean to mooch breakfast off you," Giles says but keeps shoveling in the food. "I just had to come over and make sure you were okay."

"I'm great." Breena smiles brightly. "Thank you for checking, though. It's sweet of you."

"Sweet of me," Giles mutters and shakes his head.

"Was it *not* sweet?" I ask and tip my head to the side, fascinated by the two of them. The push and pull between them is just...sexy as hell.

"I think it's sweet." Lorelei gives Giles a smile that has the man narrowing his eyes behind his black-rimmed glasses.

"We're meeting with the others tonight," Breena says, doing her best to ignore all of us. "Samhain is only two days away. It makes sense that things are starting to ramp up and get creepier. Something is trying to scare us."

"Doing a good job of it, too," Giles mutters.

"I didn't like that walk home last night," I agree. "The air was just...*charged* with something that didn't feel right."

"It's been that way for days," Giles says and pushes away his empty plate.

"You know, we'd usually be getting ready for fun parties in town and our coven celebration for Samhain. This year, we're trying to stop evil and lift a curse," Lorelei says. "There's never a dull moment around here."

"It's not funny," Giles says, but his hands have

stopped shaking, and his eyes don't look quite so drawn. "All three of you could be at risk."

"I'm the one it's targeted this year," I remind him, but Giles shakes his head.

"We don't know that for certain," he says. "Yes, you're the one it's messed with the most, but it could be smoke and mirrors for all we know."

"Well, I'm glad that we're meeting with the others tonight." Breena nods. "I'm going to bring a big charcuterie board with me. I think that sounds easy and fun."

I press my lips together so I don't giggle when Giles just stares at Breena as if she just said she'd like to commit arson on her way to the meeting.

"You're thinking about *food*?" he demands.

"I mean, I mostly only think about food," Lorelei says. "So I appreciate a good charcuterie board."

"Same," I agree with a nod. "I'll bring some edible flowers from the garden to make it extra pretty."

"Oh, how lovely," Breena says with a grin. "I love that."

"We're discussing murder tonight," Giles reminds the room. "In case anyone forgot."

"We have to eat," Breena says with patience. "It might as well be pretty food."

"Sure, why not?" Giles asks. "Should we dress up, too? I probably have a tux shoved in the back of my closet from someone's wedding ten years ago."

"That would be nice," Breena replies, and Lorelei and I have to cover our mouths with our hands to keep from cackling. "From what I remember, you look handsome in a tux."

"You're kidding, right?"

Breena simply smiles serenely, and Giles swears under his breath. "Thanks for the pancakes," he mutters as he stands.

"You're welcome." Breena follows him to the door, and before he can walk outside, she tugs on his arm to stop him. "Thank you. Seriously, thank you for coming to check on me this morning. It means a lot."

"I came for myself as much as for you." He pulls her in once more, but the hug is gentler now, less urgent.

No less sweet, though.

"I'm okay," I hear Breena whisper against his chest. "See you later."

With that, Giles nods and leaves, and when Breena closes the door behind him, she leans against it and closes her eyes.

"Holy shit, Breen," I say with a big grin. "You're having a romance with *Giles*."

But when she opens her eyes, my smile fades.

Tears spill over onto her cheeks, and she quickly wipes at them as if she's embarrassed and doesn't want us to see.

"What's wrong?" Lorelei asks, sitting up at attention.

"Nothing," she says, but the sniffle gives her away.

"Right. Because we always cry when Giles leaves a room." I frown at Breena and cross my arms over my chest. "Did he whisper something to you that you didn't like?"

"Do we have to beat him up?" Lorelei demands.

"No." Breena sighs and then lowers herself into a chair, looking defeated. "He didn't do anything, and it *was* sweet that he came to check on me."

"So why the tears?"

Breena sniffles once more and then turns her gaze on the window. "Because although I've had a crush on him forever, I know in my heart that he's not meant for me. And it just hurts."

"Breena, you don't know that," Lorelei says, but Breena shakes her head sharply.

"Stop." Her voice is hard. "Don't placate me. I know what I know. And I'll be fine, but I want just one stupid moment where I get to cry over it a little."

"Then you should cry," I say softly and reach over to take her hand. "If that's what you need to do, then do it."

CHAPTER TWENTY
JONAS

The illness seems to have finally passed.

It's almost noon when I knock on Louisa's door. The rest of the coven is recovering nicely, with no fevers, healthy appetites, and color in their cheeks.

It was a long night—perhaps the longest of my life—but I'm relieved that the worst seems to be over.

John answers the door, looking rested and happy today.

"Good morning, Jonas."

"From the look of things, you both had a better night."

The other man nods and closes the door behind me. "She has improved so much. I told her she should rest and not cook the midday meal, but she insisted."

"I feel well enough to dance," Louisa says with a

bright smile, but when her eyes meet mine, I see the worry in them. "We have things to discuss."

"I believe we do."

And I'm so grateful that I have the opportunity to talk with my old friend that I'm afraid I might cry.

"Come." Louisa points to a chair. John kisses his wife on the cheek before leaving the house to see to matters outside. I suspect they arranged this before I arrived. "There is time while the chicken cooks. How much time has passed since we cast the curse, Jonas?"

Louisa watches me with sober, concerned eyes.

"More than three hundred years," I reply with a sigh.

Louisa sits back, stunned, and then tears fill her eyes. "*What*? Jonas, how? How is that possible? It was only supposed to be a couple of years, at the most. Hallows End hasn't changed."

"We're in a bubble," I remind her, and her gaze falls to my lips.

"Your speech is different."

"A little," I admit. "There's so much to tell you, and I can't even begin to explain how much I've missed talking with you, my friend."

"Tell me everything." She leans forward again, eager to hear what I have to say. "Start at the beginning."

And so, I do. I tell Louisa everything that's happened since that night so long ago when we cast the curse. And when I've finished, she wipes at the tears falling down her cheeks.

"I knew the burden would be too great," she says at

last, shaking her head. "Jonas, you have essentially been alone for three centuries."

"But I found my soul mate," I remind her gently. "It took a long time, but I found her, and that makes all of this worth it."

"I would like to meet her," she says with a smile. "If she has captured your heart so completely, she must be a special woman."

"She is incredible," I agree. "I think you would be good friends. She owns an apothecary store, and you would *love* the wares she carries there."

"Oh, that sounds wonderful. I cannot help but wonder...if I can now remember what happened, has the curse been lifted?"

"You are the only one who remembers." My voice is quiet. "I have been with the others all night, and no one else mentioned it at all."

She closes her eyes, her face stricken with an expression of grief.

"When you had the fever before, you said that in order to break the curse, we needed a sacrifice. What did you mean by that?"

"I do not know." She opens her eyes again. "It might have been a nightmare from the fever. Jonas, I have to give you something. You should have had it long ago, as it might have aided you."

She hurries to her bedroom and then returns, carrying a slim box.

"It is a wand that once belonged to my mother. I

know that not all witches use such tools, but this one holds great magic. Take it."

"Are you certain?"

"I have no doubt," she confirms. "I feel that you will be able to use it."

"Thank you. I will keep it safe and return it to you when this is all finished."

"I have no doubt of that either. You will prevail, Jonas."

I open the box and study the wand, feeling the magic coming from it.

"Perhaps we should gather the rest of the coven and tell them, Louisa. Explain it all to them. Maybe that will help me lift the curse."

She suddenly looks confused, her gaze unfocused.

She blinks and frowns. "Tell them what? Oh, hello, Jonas. How lovely to see you. Will you join us for the midday meal?"

No.

Goddess, no.

Just like that, my dear friend has slipped away again.

I want to scream, but I simply smile and stand from the table, kissing the top of her head.

"No, thank you. I must go. Have a good day, Louisa."

"You, as well."

I leave her house and walk down the dirt road to my cabin. Once inside, I set the wand on a bookshelf, then gather some things to take to Lucy's with me.

I'm coming back.

Good. I miss you. I'm at the shop with Nera.

Anticipation fills me as I leave my cabin and walk toward the bridge. Lucy will soothe my raw nerves with her gentle touch and sweet smile.

I need to see my wife.

"So, a child has been born, and an illness rolled through the entire coven, all in the past few days," Xander says, tapping his fingertips on the table thoughtfully.

All six of us are back at his house, gathered in his library.

"I feel like this is all a game." Giles shakes his head in agitation. "Like something is just playing with us. Playing a game of cat and mouse, chasing us around and trying to confuse us."

"That could certainly be the case," Xander says with a slow nod, reaching for some cheese and crackers on the tray of food that Breena brought with her to share.

"Are the two connected?" Lorelei asks and then holds up her hands. "Just hear me out. Could the annual murders of witches be connected to the curse of the blood moon? We've been tackling them separately, but what if they're linked?"

"We haven't thought of it like that," Lucy says but sighs when Xander doesn't say anything. "You did."

"I considered it," he agrees. "But even with all the research I've done, I can't find any evidence that that's the case. It doesn't mean that Lorelei isn't correct, of course."

"It's just that we don't have evidence, and no reason to think they're the same," Lorelei says. "I was really hoping to kill two birds with one stone."

"That would be convenient," I reply with a smile. "And I wish it were the case, but I can tell you that I'd never even heard of the murders until I met you."

"It's so odd to me that you never heard of it from the newspapers or anywhere else in all these years," Breena says. "The cases are open, and most have gone cold."

"We may be several hundred years out from the persecution of witches," Giles says, "but that doesn't mean law enforcement busts their asses to figure out the deaths of witches. Besides, in most cases, it's looked like suicide."

"Come on," Lucy says, getting agitated with anger. She rubs her hands down her thighs as if they're suddenly sweaty. "One witch found dead every Samhain is not freaking suicide."

"What if those looking into it are under a spell?" Breena asks, speaking slowly. "They aren't investigating because they *can't*."

"Interesting," I murmur. "And quite possible."

"Do you see that?" Lorelei asks Lucy as she points at the window. We all look that way, but I don't see anything aside from the darkening sky.

"I see it," Breena confirms. Her voice trembles, and Lucy immediately reaches for my hand.

"Oh, shit," she murmurs.

"I don't see anything," Giles says.

"I don't either," I reply.

Xander, with his eyes narrowed, walks to the window and stares out. "What do you see, ladies?"

"A man," Lorelei says and joins him at the window. Xander links their hands, and Lorelei doesn't pull away. "He's standing on the sidewalk, watching us."

"He's creepy as hell," Lucy adds. "He looks...*dead*."

"How so?" I ask her.

"Rotting flesh," Breena answers. "Dirty. He looks like a zombie out of a movie. It's really cliché, actually."

"He might very well *be* dead," Xander replies calmly.

"Do you see it, Xander?" Giles asks.

"No. It seems that whatever it is, it wants to frighten our girls."

"It's working." Breena shudders. "And now it's *smiling*. It still has all its teeth, though. So, a zombie with good dental hygiene?"

I narrow my eyes. I want to see it, to try to understand what's trying to harm these women, but when I look outside, there's no one there.

"Skinwalker," I whisper, and Xander nods.

"It's likely."

"It's the eyes that creep me out," Lucy says.

"We're only a few hours from Samhain now." Lorelei looks up at Xander. "And it's getting braver."

"It can't get inside," Breena points out. "It can't get to us in here or in any of our homes."

"It got to *me* in mine," Lucy reminds her. "After we had worked some pretty powerful magic."

"It's gone," Lorelei says in surprise, pointing. "It's just...*gone.*"

"What the hell?" Lucy asks. "I think I trusted it more when I could see it."

"This is evil on a whole new level." Xander reluctantly lets go of Lorelei's hand and returns to his seat.

"I admit, even what I went through in New Orleans didn't scare me quite this badly, and that was pretty fucking terrifying."

"We stay together," Breena insists. "Like Lorelei said, it's only a few more hours until midnight, and that's when it always happens, between midnight and morning. I'm not losing any of you to this sick son of a bitch."

"Wow, you *never* swear," Lorelei says and then pats Breena on the shoulder. "Good job."

"I'm *so* mad." Breena scowls down at her hands. "I've never been this pissed off."

I narrow my eyes at her. "*Never?*"

"No." She stands and starts to pace the room, her blond hair swirling around her shoulders as she moves back and forth, anger coming off her in waves. "I want to punch something. Hard."

"This is...different," Lucy says thoughtfully.

She's not herself, she says only to me.

I share a look with Xander, and he nods once.

It seems this particular evil *can* come inside.

"Breena, why don't you sit down?" Xander asks softly. "I'll pour you some whiskey."

"I don't want your fucking *whiskey*," she shouts as she rounds on him. "I don't want anything from *you*, except for all of you to just leave me alone. Just leave me the fuck alone!"

She rushes out of the room, and Giles immediately runs after her.

"It has her." I have to work to keep my voice calm.

"We have to get it *out* of her," Lucy says urgently. "Why are we sitting here?"

"I have her!" Giles shouts from the other room. "Hurry!"

Xander grabs my sister's Book of Shadows, and we run to the living room, where Giles is holding a snarling Breena.

"Cast the circle," Xander says as Lorelei and Lucy immediately begin to pour salt around Giles and Breena, and Xander starts chanting an old, simple spell that I remember hearing when I was a child.

I join him, remembering the words.

Evil be gone, washed clean away, leave this witch free of affliction today.

Over and over again, we repeat the spell, until Breena coughs, gasps, and then falls limp in Giles's grip.

She's sweaty but breathing and conscious.

"What in the world?" she asks as she looks up at Giles.

"You had an intruder," he informs her. "But it's been evicted."

"I feel so cold." She burrows against him. "Will you please take me home? I want to get under the covers and warm up."

"I have a guest room here," Xander says, but she shakes her head.

"I really want my own house," she insists. "With my things. I'll feel better."

"I'll take her," Giles says. "And I'll stay with her."

"We will all come to you," Xander decides. "I don't want anyone alone tonight. We're safer in numbers, and if this son of a bitch comes back, I want all of us together to fight it."

"You know," I say, remembering the wand that Louisa gave me earlier. "I was given a wand that once belonged to a very powerful witch. It may just help us in this fight. I left it in Hallows End, but it won't take long for me to go and get it."

"I think we need all the help we can get." Giles helps Breena to her feet. "I'll go get her settled and see you all there soon."

"Lorelei, I'd like to get some things from the shop," Lucy says. "Will you come with me?"

"I'll take you both," Xander replies and simply raises his brow at Lorelei when she starts to decline. "We can swing by your place, as well, and then go to Breena's for the night."

"I like the idea of the three of you together," I say,

agreeing with Xander. I pull Lucy to me and kiss her, hard and fast. "I won't be long."

"Just be careful." She clings to me. "And quick. Because I'm freaked out."

"I'll hurry," I assure her.

I ride with the others as far as Lucy's house and then, after agreeing to see them at Breena's shortly, I hurry to the bridge and cross into Hallows End.

It's not quiet in the village tonight as everyone celebrates Samhain—as they always do, every month without fail.

I hurry to my cabin and find the wand right where I left it earlier today, then turn to return to Salem.

But when I arrive at the foot of the bridge, I hit a wall.

I can't move forward.

I can't cross back into the modern day, back to Lucy.

I narrow my eyes and reach out with just my hand, but it's like touching ice-cold glass.

"Is everything well, Jonas?"

I turn to see Alistair standing not far behind me, a congenial smile on his weathered face.

"Yes, thank you. I was just thinking of a walk on this fine evening."

"Yes, 'tis a fine evening indeed. Enjoy it."

"Thank you. I hope you enjoy the festivities."

He simply shrugs. "I'm happy the others like it, but I have never been partial to the holiday. Now, Christmas is a holiday that I enjoy. It will be coming upon us soon."

"Of course." I offer him a smile, and Alistair nods and then walks back into the village.

When I turn to the bridge again, I'm still trapped, unable to cross.

Where are you? Lucy's voice sounds frustrated.

Working on getting back. I seem to have hit a snag.

She's quiet for a moment. *What kind of snag?*

I'm trapped, Lucy.

CHAPTER TWENTY-ONE

The plan is coming together perfectly. Perhaps, rather than just one, there will be three this time.

Chapter Twenty-Two
Lucy

What do you mean, you're trapped?

But now, there's no response from Jonas at all.

"Jonas says he can't get back here," I announce, hearing the panic in my voice. "Xander, he says he's trapped."

"Fuck," Xander whispers and wipes his hand down his face. "I should have anticipated this."

"How can it block him?" I ask as the frustration bubbles through me. My stomach is roiling, my breath coming fast as Lorelei drives us over to Breena's. "How, Xander?"

"I don't know," he says grimly, shaking his head. "Let me think."

I keep trying to reach out to Jonas, but all I can hear are snippets of words as if he's trying to speak to me through a cell phone and has horrible reception.

"I will *not* lose him tonight."

"We're going to figure it out," Lorelei assures me as she parks behind Breena's car in the driveway. "We'll get him here. There's just a weird blip in the matrix or something."

"This isn't a movie, Lorelei."

Nera runs ahead, anxious to make sure that his favorite person is okay.

When we walk into the house, Giles is sitting on the couch, his head in his hands. He looks up at us with haunted eyes and shakes his head.

"This is some fucked-up shit."

"Is she okay?" I ask him.

"She's sleeping. I had a hell of a time keeping her awake on the ride home. Finally, I just let her drift off and carried her to bed when we got here. She's exhausted, as if she ran a marathon or something."

"She did," Xander replies.

"Having something like that inside your head is exhausting," I confirm. "And scary. I understand why she wanted to come home to sleep. Breena has always been one to want comfort."

"I wanted to stay with her, to lie down with her, but it felt like an intrusion, so I came out here. And that pisses me off, too."

"Why?"

"Because if she'd just talk to me, *listen* to me, we'd be together, and I wouldn't feel like a damn outsider in her bedroom."

"It's not the time for that," Xander says. His voice is firm but not unkind. "I know you're impatient, but the time will come, Giles."

I try to reach out for Jonas, but there's still nothing. Not even the static anymore.

"I've lost my tether to Jonas." I can hear the quaver in my voice. "For the goddess's sake, Xander, he could be in danger there."

"This is where we remind you," Lorelei says, "that Jonas is a powerful, centuries-old witch who can absolutely handle himself. Lucy, he's not powerless or weak."

"I *know* that." My frustration is only growing, and I'm agitated. "Jonas can handle anything that comes at him. But, damn it, I love him, and I'm freaking out here."

"Where is she?" Hilda bursts into the room with Astrid close on her heels. "Where's my baby?"

"She's in her room, asleep," Giles says, but Hilda shakes her head and runs through the house to Breena's bedroom.

"It has her!" Hilda yells and bursts into Breena's room.

All of us are knocked back on our butts from the force coming through the doorway.

Standing in the middle of the room in nothing but a sheer nightgown is Breena.

Her eyes are glassy and white. Unfocused. Her blond hair billows in an unnatural breeze, and walking around her, almost ghost-like, is a man.

One I don't know or recognize.

"Breena!" Giles stands and tries to walk into the room, but it's as though the doorway is covered in glass, and he can't get through. We can watch, we can *hear*, but we can't go inside. "Goddamn it, you motherfucker, let her go."

The man looks our way and smiles but doesn't stop doing whatever he's doing.

Jonas, where are you? We need your help!

There's no answer.

"Start the chant," Xander says. "The same one from earlier at my house."

Lorelei and I join hands, the others follow suit, and we begin the spell.

Evil be gone, washed clean away, leave this witch free of affliction today.

But after just the first time through, *he* simply laughs at us and pulls a long length of rope out of a bag, beginning to loop it over the chandelier in the bedroom.

"Help me," Breena croaks.

"Godsdamn it," Giles mutters and tries to break through the door again, failing. "Get me in there, Xander."

"Not my baby," Hilda whispers. "No, not my baby."

I glance over and see my mother standing with her sisters, and when her eyes meet mine, they're full of grief and sadness as if she knows *he* will be successful.

"No," I say, shaking my head. "Mom, what do we do?"

"Hold on." Lorelei takes a deep breath before lifting her arms and beginning the recitation of a broken barriers spell.

We join in, and that gives the evil pause. He frowns over at us, and when the barrier is broken, Giles bursts through, and Breena begins to scream.

"HELP ME! GILES! HELP ME!"

But the evil raises a hand, and Giles goes flying backward, hitting the wall.

We're all in the room now, but we can't get close to her. We're unable to move.

With us at bay, he returns to his task of fastening the rope into a noose and slipping it over Breena's head.

"NO!" she screams, over and over again. "I do not receive this. I do *not* receive this."

With a flash of light, my mom whips into the room and attacks the evil, knocking him back.

His face crumples in fury, and he lashes out at her, leaving Breena huddled on the floor, the noose still around her neck.

"I can't get to you, baby," Giles says, even speaking seeming to take great effort. "I'm trying, but it has me trapped."

"Don't want to die," Breena whispers as her white eyes focus on something on the floor. "Don't want to go so soon."

The evil throws Mom out the window, but she flies back in again, her teeth bared and eyes red, ready to kick some ass.

But the evil draws in a deep breath and then screams in a wail so sharp and shrill we all try to cover our ears.

My mother disappears.

CHAPTER TWENTY-THREE
JONAS

The scream pulls me out of my panic, acting like a slap across the face while drowning.

I scowl and look around, but I can't see where it came from, and then the mark on my hand begins to burn.

I take a breath, close my eyes, and feel the power within me build, starting at my sacral chakra and moving up like a fire.

"*Fire.*"

I open my eyes, stare at the wall of energy keeping me away from Lucy, and know immediately what I have to do.

I remove the wand from the box and, with my hands up above my head, raise my voice.

Eyes wide open, elements rise,
Power and might from earth to skies,
Build within to use without,

Remove all hindrance, erase all doubt.
Let me pass from here to thee,
This is my will, so mote it be!

Fire builds in the center of the energy, unlike any fire I've ever lit or kindled before. This is fiercely blue, starts small, and then spreads.

I can't hear Lucy's thoughts, but I can feel the chaos around her. I can feel the fear and worry. The grief. I use that energy to fuel mine, making the fire grow bigger and brighter.

You will not keep me from that I love,
You have no power here.
I will defeat thee from below and above,
This fire will scorch and sear.

I push against the heat of the fire and the energy trying to hold me in with all my might. At last, I break through and am able to run across the bridge.

I don't stop until I reach Breena's house. Lightning flashes above and around her little home, and I can feel the chaos inside.

I run in, relieved to see Lucy standing, but then come to an abrupt halt when I see the man standing behind Breena.

"Alistair?"

All eyes turn to me, and Lucy cries out in relief, but I can't take my eyes off the man from Hallows End.

"Alistair?" I repeat.

"Nooooo." His voice slithers like a snake over my skin, and I watch in disgust as his hands roam over

Breena's body. She's as pale as death, her eyes white the way Lucy's were the night her house was destroyed, and Breena doesn't put up a fight when Alistair starts to pull on the rope, lifting her heels off the floor.

She struggles to keep her toes planted on the ground as Giles struggles to free himself from invisible shackles, desperate to get to Breena.

"Alistair," I repeat and step toward him, but he turns to me and screams, the same one I heard in Hallows End. I'm trapped.

"You have the wand," Xander says, yelling over the wind that's picked up in the room. "Use the wand, Jonas."

It takes all my might to point it at Alistair and begin speaking. At first, he ignores me and simply lifts Breena off her feet. She's dangling now, twitching as her body fights for air.

As I speak, my voice grows louder and weakens the bonds keeping me prisoner. The others are able to move, as well, and we all start to speak as one.

Alistair turns to us, his black eyes wide, his mouth gaping inhumanly wide as he screams.

Mist leaves his body, floating up to the ceiling, and then, still shrieking, it flies out the window and into the darkness.

Alistair's body crumples to the floor as we all race to Breena, who also fell.

Giles scoops her into his arms, crying as he checks for a pulse.

"Damn it," he mutters. "Breena, you can't leave me like this. Damn it, Breena."

But when he looks up at us, I know.

There's no pulse.

"No," Hilda cries and kneels next to Giles, pulling her child into her arms. "No, no, no, my sweet girl. My darling baby."

I turn to Alistair, who is moaning and rolling on the floor. When he opens his eyes, they fill with terror as he skitters back against the wall.

"Help me." His throat sounds raw. "Where am I? Please, help me."

"He doesn't know," Xander says.

"No." My voice is grim as Xander lays a hand over Alistair's forehead and puts him to sleep. "It used Alistair to do its bidding. Though how it took a man from Hallows End and brought him here, I have no idea."

"Breena!"

Giles has the woman by the shoulders as she gasps for breath, her green eyes wide and hands pulling at the rope still around her neck.

"Get it off," Lorelei says, yanking on the rope herself. "Oh, thank the goddess, the ward worked."

Breena still gasps, her eyes pinned to Giles as he breathes with her, trying to calm her down.

Lucy throws herself into my arms and holds on tightly, her arms trembling around my neck.

"Jonas," she whispers. "Oh, goddess, Jonas. I thought I'd lost you."

"I was trapped," I reply and breathe her in. "But I got out. Nothing can ever keep me from you, my love."

"She needs a hospital," Giles says as he lifts Breena into his arms.

"No," Breena wheezes. "No hospital."

"You *absolutely* need a hospital," he disagrees.

I squeeze Lucy and whisper in her ear, "One moment, sweetheart."

"Jonas can help me," Breena says and smiles sweetly at Giles. "I promise."

Giles lays her on the bed and refuses to leave her side as I move over to examine her. To my astonishment, the ligature marks around her neck have already begun to fade. The bruises where the evil hit her are also lightening, and she seems to be breathing just fine.

"She's recovering quickly." I smile down at her. "How do you feel, Breena?"

"Oh, I'll need therapy for sure," she says. "But I think I'm okay—physically, anyway."

"She'll need a few hours to get back to herself," Lucy adds from behind me. "Been there."

I place my hands on her chest and close my eyes. I feel the fire build within me and push the energy into Breena. She takes a deep breath, accepting it, and when I pull back, she smiles.

"You really *are* a healer."

"I really am."

"Oh, darling," Hilda says, taking her daughter's hand. "I'm so proud of you."

"I literally did *nothing*." Breena looks at Giles. "Thank you."

He licks his lips, shakes his head, and leaves the room.

"I guess he's mad at me," Breena says.

"I'd say he needs a minute to himself," Xander replies. "I think we've all had enough work for one night. But we do need to meet soon. We defeated it tonight, but not for always."

"Agreed," I reply with a nod. "It will return next year at this time. And it will be angry."

"We'll be ready," Lucy says. Her eyes narrow, and she points at Alistair. "In the meantime, what do we do about him? And who is he?"

"He's the mayor of Hallows End," I reply. "I'll take him back."

"No." Lucy grips my hand fiercely. "You're *not* going back there. Absolutely not."

I pull her against me and brush my fingers down her cheek, smiling down into her gorgeous green eyes.

"*Nothing* can keep me from you, my love. I'll take him home and be right back."

"We'll want to make sure he doesn't remember," Xander adds. "For his own sanity."

"I'll take care of it," I reply without pulling my gaze away from Lucy's. "I promise, I'll be right back. And I don't make promises lightly."

"No." She lifts onto her toes so she can press her lips to mine. "You don't."

With Alistair tucked in bed and oblivious to what happened just hours ago in Breena's house, I walk through Hallows End.

Rebecca Akerman walks out of her cabin to fetch some water from her well.

Her belly is round with pregnancy.

She waves at me with a smile and then returns inside with a full bucket of water.

There are clouds overhead, sending down a drizzle of rain, and as I stand in my little village, I know without a shadow of a doubt that everything has been reset.

To the way it's always been since the night, exactly three-hundred and thirty-one years ago, that I placed the curse of the blood moon and set these things in motion.

We didn't lift the curse tonight.

And while we did prevail over evil, we didn't destroy it.

But for now, everything is calm.

I turn to cross the bridge and do so easily without any barrier. The walk through the woods is one I know very well.

And when the trees part, and I see Lucy kneeling in her garden with Nera by her side, I smile.

For now, I live in two times. Two homes.

And I'm grateful.

Lucy's head turns as if she senses me, and when she sees me, she smiles and stands to greet me.

"Everything okay over there?"

"For now." I kiss her lightly and let my hands roam up and down her slim back. Nera bumps my hip, looking for an ear scratch, and I oblige him.

"We've been invited to celebrate with the coven tomorrow. They'll want to see for themselves that we're all safe."

"I think that sounds like a good idea. Lucy, have the aunts seen your mother?"

Agatha disappeared during her fight with the darkness, and I feared that she'd be gone for good.

But Lucy's face lights up. "Yes. She's back at the cottage, where she should be."

I sigh in relief. I know that we have so much work ahead of us. We need to find the answers to so many questions, but for now, everyone is safe.

"Let's go inside," she suggests. "Rest."

"Come on, boy." I gesture for Nera to follow us. "We all deserve some rest."

CHAPTER TWENTY-FOUR

The energy is gone. He's exiled once again, locked away where he will heal and slowly regain the parts of him they disbursed.

It will take time.

But he has all the time in the world.

And when he's recovered, he won't stop at just one.

He will kill them all.

Are you ready to find out what happens next in The Curse of the Blood Moon series? Breena and Giles are next in Cauldrons Call. You can get all of the information here:

https://www.kristenprobyauthor.com/cauldrons-call

About the Author

Kristen Proby has published more than sixty titles, many of which have hit the USA Today, New York Times and Wall Street Journal Bestsellers lists.

Kristen and her husband, John, make their home in her hometown of Whitefish, Montana with their two cats and dog.

facebook.com/booksbykristenproby

instagram.com/kristenproby

bookbub.com/profile/kristen-proby

goodreads.com/kristenproby

Newsletter Sign Up

I hope you enjoyed reading this story as much as I enjoyed writing it! For upcoming book news, be sure to join my newsletter! I promise I will only send you news-filled mail, and none of the spam. You can sign up here:

https://mailchi.mp/kristenproby.com/newsletter-sign-up

ALSO BY KRISTEN PROBY:

Other Books by Kristen Proby

The Single in Seattle Series
The Secret
The Surprise
The Scandal

The With Me In Seattle Series

Come Away With Me
Under The Mistletoe With Me
Fight With Me
Play With Me
Rock With Me
Safe With Me
Tied With Me

Breathe With Me

Forever With Me

Stay With Me

Indulge With Me

Love With Me

Dance With Me

Dream With Me

You Belong With Me

Imagine With Me

Shine With Me

Escape With Me

Flirt With Me

Change With Me

Take a Chance With Me

Check out the full series here: https://www.
kristenprobyauthor.com/with-me-in-seattle

The Big Sky Universe

Love Under the Big Sky
Loving Cara
Seducing Lauren
Falling for Jillian
Saving Grace

The Big Sky
Charming Hannah

Kissing Jenna
Waiting for Willa
Soaring With Fallon

Big Sky Royal
Enchanting Sebastian
Enticing Liam
Taunting Callum

Heroes of Big Sky
Honor
Courage
Shelter

Check out the full Big Sky universe here: https://
www.kristenprobyauthor.com/under-the-big-sky

Bayou Magic
Shadows
Spells
Serendipity

Check out the full series here: https://www.
kristenprobyauthor.com/bayou-magic

The Romancing Manhattan Series

All the Way

All it Takes
After All

Check out the full series here: https://www.kristenprobyauthor.com/romancing-manhattan

The Boudreaux Series

Easy Love
Easy Charm
Easy Melody
Easy Kisses
Easy Magic
Easy Fortune
Easy Nights

Check out the full series here: https://www.kristenprobyauthor.com/boudreaux

The Fusion Series

Listen to Me
Close to You
Blush for Me
The Beauty of Us
Savor You

Check out the full series here: https://www.kristenprobyauthor.com/fusion

From 1001 Dark Nights

Easy With You
Easy For Keeps
No Reservations
Tempting Brooke
Wonder With Me
Shine With Me

Kristen Proby's Crossover Collection

Soaring with Fallon, A Big Sky Novel

Wicked Force: A Wicked Horse Vegas/Big Sky Novella
By Sawyer Bennett

All Stars Fall: A Seaside Pictures/Big Sky Novella
By Rachel Van Dyken

Hold On: A Play On/Big Sky Novella
By Samantha Young

Worth Fighting For: A Warrior Fight Club/Big Sky
Novella
By Laura Kaye

Crazy Imperfect Love: A Dirty Dicks/Big Sky Novella
By K.L. Grayson

Nothing Without You: A Forever Yours/Big Sky Novella
By Monica Murphy

Check out the entire Crossover Collection here:
https://www.kristenprobyauthor.com/kristen-proby-crossover-collection